TANGLING WITH THE ALPHA

WOLF SHIFTER FAIRY TALE RETELLINGS
BOOK THREE

BELLA MOONDRAGON

For Ms. Davis—but I still hate math.

CONTENTS

THE TOWER IN THE FOREST

Leo

The wind shifts the moment I step outside, laced with pine, smoke, and something darker stirring beneath it all. I pause at the threshold, my eyes sweeping the horizon as the trees whisper in an uneasy rhythm. My instincts have kept me on edge for days now—something is undeniably wrong.

Marek finds me before I call for him. He's always been two steps ahead.

"We need to talk," he says without preamble.

I nod and jerk my head toward the fire pit. It's unlit, but the circle of stone feels like the perfect ground for discussing strategy.

We sit across from each other, both of us still in human form, though I feel the wolf pacing beneath my skin. He does too—I can see it in the way his jaw clenches, in the tension vibrating through his shoulders.

"He should've been back by now," I say.

Marek doesn't flinch. "Missing three days."

I grit my teeth. "Too long."

"Just a standard sweep past the ridge, chasing fresh elk tracks. We both cleared the route ourselves last week. There were no signs of danger."

"How many returned home?" I ask.

"Three. Corwin leading, plus Kianna and Harla."

My chest tightens. "And there's been no word from Silas at all?"

Marek meets my eyes and shakes his head again. "None. It was his first real hunt. He's quick, Leo, and smart."

"Too young." I exhale slowly. "He wasn't ready."

"You know Corwin wouldn't have brought him if he didn't believe he could handle it."

"I trust Corwin," I say. "But that doesn't change the fact that Silas has vanished."

Marek shifts from one foot to the other, his brows furrowed. "Corwin said they ran into trouble."

"Rogues?"

"Yes. He said that an ambush split them up during their hunt."

"And that was the last they saw of him?"

He nods. "Silas could've been hurt."

I stand abruptly, pacing in a slow circle as the wind shifts again. Smoke. Earth. Faint traces of a rainstorm.

"I should've gone with them."

"You're the Alpha," Marek says. "You can't go chasing every hunting party."

"No, but maybe I should've sent someone else with more experience. Silas is just a kid."

"He's twenty-one. He's reckless, but he has to learn. You were leading hunts at that age."

"That was different," I snap. "I didn't have a choice."

Marek doesn't argue. He lets the silence sit between us for a beat, heavy and tense.

I stare out at the tree line, the long dark veil of the forest creeping toward the edge of our land. My pulse hammers. Whoever dared to attack my hunters, whoever took one of my pack members, they've made a fatal mistake.

"I'll lead a search team tonight. I want every stone, root, and den between here and the ridge searched."

"Yes, Alpha."

"If Silas's alive, we bring him home."

"And if he's not?" Marek asks, his voice soft.

I meet his gaze without blinking. "Then we bring back his body, and we make them pay."

Marek nods once, sharp and solemn. He rises with me, and we turn together to face the forest.

The sun is just beginning to set when the search begins. I smell the rain rolling in as we cross the ridge, the forest humming with tension.

My wolf strains beneath my skin, uneasy. I shift.

It's been days since the hunting party left Moon River, and now one of our own is missing. A young wolf named Silas, barely past his first shift.

I should've gone with them.

Instead, Marek and I are here now, with three of our best scouts, Tarin, Briar, and Zekia. We cut through the underbrush as thunder rumbles, mere miles away. The storm is closing in fast. Leaves shiver overhead, and the air carries the first hints of rain.

"He was last seen near here," Briar says beside me, through the mind-link. "They fought off the rogues. He was bleeding when he ran."

"Bleeding and alone," I reply. We can see all the signs.

Zekia, walking just ahead, growls low in his throat before adding, "It's not like Silas to run. The fight must have left him injured and separated him from the others.

The forest floor bears silent witness—upturned soil where paws skidded, deep gouges in the bark of a nearby cedar, still weeping sap. Broken underbrush forms a chaotic trail, flecked here and there with rust-colored drops that cling to leaves like dew.

"There's blood on the lower branches," Briar says, nudging one with her snout.

"And the scent trail cuts east, sharp, like he panicked," I note. "He was running full speed."

"Whatever happened back there, it scattered them hard," Zekia adds.

"Either way, we find him before nightfall," I say. "Or we double the search at first light."

Lightning streaks across the sky, silver veins against a deepening bruise of midnight blue cloud. The forest darkens unnaturally quickly, as though the sun's been snuffed out moments too early.

Raindrops, fast and fierce, crash through the canopy with sudden violence, soaking us in seconds. We press forward, the mud sucking at our paws. Branches whip as the storm howls through the trees.

"We need to find cover!" Tarin says.

"Go northeast," I call back. "There's a cave not too far. I'll circle wide—check the ridge for tracks and catch up with you."

"Alpha—" Briar starts, but I cut her off.

"Go!" I turn and veer off alone, the storm swallowing the others in seconds.

The forest twists around me, slick and shadowed. Every step is a battle against roots and rain. I move low, close to the ground, my eyes sharp for any sign, broken branches, paw prints, blood. But the storm has already wiped most of it clean.

I should turn back.

But something tugs at me. It's a faint scent, strange, sweet, and alive. I follow it, my ears flat, tail down, pushing deeper into the trees until they thicken and crowd together like a wall.

Before me, a curtain of vines sways gently, stirred by the breeze, like it's hiding something enchanted just out of reach. My Alpha instincts draw me closer.

The vines seem too uniform, too deliberately arranged across the rocky slope to be natural. I notice the scent is stronger here, lush and wild, like honey warmed by sunlight. I feel as though spring itself could be waiting on the other side.

I push through, and the moment I step beyond the vines, the storm vanishes.

No rain. No lightning. No thunder.

Just the last streaks of sunlight before it dips behind the peaks.

I stumble forward, blinking hard, disoriented. The air is warm and still, scented with buttercups and ripe fruit. I turn in a slow circle.

A valley stretches out before me, broad and untouched. Towering mountains cradle it on all sides, their tops dusted in snow. Birds call lazily overhead, a brook gurgles nearby, and the grass is emerald green.

I've found the secret Moonbeam Valley....

With caution, I move forward, my ears tuned for danger, but the valley greets me like an old friend. Bees drift lazily, dipping into blossoms. Trees heavy with peaches and lemons bow gently.

I reach the brook and drink; the crystal-clear water is cold and sweet. Instantly, I feel something uncoil in my chest, like I've never truly breathed until now.

There's no trace of Silas or rogues here. Passersby usually cannot find this place, but tonight, the valley is revealing itself to me.

The Moon Goddess Herself protects these sacred lands; I feel it in my bones. And tonight it's like the land is watching me and deciding whether I belong.

I stand and look back toward the vine wall. It's still there, rippling, and the forest waits beyond, dark, wild, and wet.

But in here... it's another world.

I should turn back. I need to find the others, to tell them where I am. But instinct tells me if I leave without understanding this place, I might never find it again.

So I wait.

Just a few more minutes, I tell myself. Long enough to understand what I've walked into.

The valley is still, and I feel as though it's listening.

And so I listen, too.

The sun slips behind the mountains entirely, and golden light fades to violet dusk. As the first stars appear, the valley changes. It doesn't dim or dull. It glows.

The flowers shimmer in radiant purples and luminous pinks, their petals glowing faintly as if lit from within. The brook dances over smooth stones, its song clear and chime-like, echoing from the surrounding mountain walls. Overhead, the breath of the valley weaves through the trees in a gentle, melodic hum, as though the forest itself is singing some forgotten lullaby.

The air feels... enchanted, mystical, alive. I pad deeper into the valley.

My senses sharpen with every leaf rustle, every root beneath the soil. The ground here is soft, and the earth carries no scent of rot, no predator trails. Just bluebells, daisies, moss, and something faint and feminine—lavender and honey. Unmistakable. Familiar.

I follow the scent, weaving between moonlit ferns and leaning trees until I reach a clearing I somehow didn't notice before.

And there it is.

A tower.

Tall and narrow, built of old stone with ivy creeping up one side. The walls gleam faintly in the moonlight. There's only one window— high above, round and arched, its wooden shutters thrown open to the night. A line stretches out from it, tied to the nearest tree, and on it hang linens, swaying in the breeze.

Who lives here?

This valley remains isolated. Hidden. I couldn't find this place again if I tried—and yet someone lives here. Someone who washes laundry and hangs it to dry under the moon.

Something about the tower seems odd to me, not that I think it's haunted or cursed. It's too calm for that. Too serene. And that's what bothers me. There's no door, and there are no stairs. Just smooth stone stretching from the grassy earth all the way to that single window as though someone built it never intending for anyone to leave.

I circle it methodically. The ivy climbs thickest near the back, but even here, there are no cracks, no hinges, no seams. No entrance. Only the faint scent again: honey and lavender, trailing like a ribbon from the open window above.

There's no light inside, but the laundry on the line tells me it's not empty. I see gowns, plain shifts, a worn apron.

I scan the treetops. Nothing stirs. No movement from the

window. No voice. Only silence, broken by the distant call of a nightbird.

Whatever this place is, it's not right, and whoever lives here is not completely alone.

I curl up under a nearby tree. My pack won't find me tonight, not in this place.

So I'll wait.

Wait and watch.

The moon climbs higher, casting silver across the clearing. The laundry sways in the wind like ghostly hands waving from above, but the tower doesn't move.

Yet, I swear I can feel it watching me.

I lower my head onto my paws, my eyes never leaving that single open window.

Who are you?

And why are you in there?

THE GIRL IN THE TOWER

Roxy

I SETTLE INTO BED, MY COMFY MATTRESS SOFT BENEATH ME. THE TOWER feels colder at night, even with the thick stone walls holding the chill at bay. I pull my blanket closer, but it barely wards off the shiver crawling down my spine.

The silence is too heavy. I should be used to it by now, but tonight, the stillness presses on me. Shadows pool on the stone floor, stretching long and dark beneath the faint moonlight streaking in through the window.

I tell myself I'm alone, and I'm safe, but the feeling that I'm being watched doesn't fade.

A flicker of movement catches my eye, a glimmer just beyond the window, or maybe inside the room....

My heart beats wild and loud. I scan the walls, the floor, the ceiling.

Nothing but stone.

I clutch the blanket tighter and pull it up to my chin, trying to summon the courage to close my eyes. Though, every creak of the tower, every whisper of the wind, sets my nerves on edge.

What if someone's out there? Watching me?

I force my breath to slow, reminding myself there is no door, there are no stairs, there are heavy curtains on the window, and it is a ridiculously high climb.

Softly, I sing a lullaby I've known since I was a child, and sleep takes me in its gentle arms.

Sleep, my light, my shining star,
No matter how far away you are.
Threads of sunlight in your hair
Weave a magic pure and rare.
Fairies will guard your sleep
And gather moonbeams in the deep.
Dreamland rivers, wild and free,
Calling you back home to me.
Though the night is deep and wide,
Love will always be your guide.
Sleep, my light, my shining star,
No matter how far away you are.
Threads of sunlight in your hair
Hold you safe with tender care.

THE NIGHT STRETCHES THIN AND FINALLY SOFTENS AS PALE LIGHT SEEPS through the window.

I know this tower better than I know myself.

The soft creak of the floorboards near the hearth. The way the breeze sings when it slips through the window. The shadows that crawl across the stone walls as the sun moves through the day. I've mapped them all, drawn them over and over again in charcoal and ink on scraps of paper.

Today is no different—at least, at first.

The cinnamon rolls rise perfectly in the oven I stoke myself. I glaze them with honey and a bit of lavender I grew from the seed pouch Mother left me months ago. I stack the fresh rolls beside the bread I baked yesterday. Next, I start a soup to simmer low and long with the last of the root vegetables. Everything smells warm and sweet.

But I don't feel well enough to enjoy any of it.

The headache starts as a twinge behind my eyes while I'm cleaning the iron pan. Then it sharpens, spreading through my skull, down my neck, and into my shoulders like something trying to claw its way out of me. I wince and drop the pan, the clang ringing through the quiet tower.

I clutch the edge of the table, unable to catch my breath. My arms tremble, and my skin feels too tight. My knees buckle, and I sink to the floor, my heart pounding.

It's not just the pain but the pressure that startles me. It's the heaviness in my bones like they're not sure what shape they're supposed to be.

"Mother," I whisper, even though I know she's not here. She hasn't been for days. She used to come home every night, but now sometimes she stays away for weeks.

I lie on the cold stone until the worst of the shaking passes. When I finally push myself upright, I'm drenched in sweat. I wipe my face with the edge of my sleeve and lean on the wall for support.

Then I hear her.

"Roxy!" comes the familiar voice, sharp as flint and firm as iron. "Let down your hair."

Relief rushes through me like spring rain. I stumble to the window seat and gather my long, heavy braid. As I ease it out the window, my fingers are clumsy, my head still pounding. My braid tumbles down, and the end disappears from sight.

Mother climbs quickly, as she always does. She's small but strong, with dark hair, sharp cheekbones, and stern gray eyes that glint like a storm before it breaks. When she swings her leg over the sill and lands beside me, her expression changes from cheerful to worrisome the instant she sees my face.

"You're pale," she says, brushing a hand across my cheek. "Sweating. Why didn't you call for me?"

"You weren't here," I murmur. "And I didn't think it was serious until—"

I hesitate. Her eyes narrow.

"Until what?"

"It feels like I'm coming apart," I whisper. "My bones ache. My skin burns. It's like something's... waking up inside me."

She pulls her hand back like I burned her. For a moment, she studies me like I'm a puzzle.

"Tell me everything," she says.

I tell her about the pain first. The pounding in my skull like a drum too close to my ears, the deep, aching throb in my spine and limbs, like something is stirring just beneath my skin. Then the heat, unbearable and crawling over me like a fever I can't sweat out, and how my clothes and skin feel too tight. I tell her how the tower felt suddenly smaller, like the walls were leaning in on me, the ceiling pressing down, the silence so loud it roared in my ears.

"I couldn't sit still." I explain. "I paced then collapsed. It was as if the air itself had turned against me, too thick to breathe."

But there's more I don't say. I don't tell her how I stood barefoot by the window, my forehead against the glass, and watched the trees swaying far below. Or how the sight of the lake shimmering in the distance made my heart ache in a way I couldn't explain. I don't tell her I imagined the feel of damp moss beneath my feet, or that I imagined walking straight into the forest with nothing but the wind in my hair. I don't tell her the wildest part of all, that for one dizzy moment, I thought I could smell the world outside the tower, and it smelled like freedom.

But maybe I don't have to. She seems to sense it.

"You mustn't go outside," she says, her voice tight. "Not now. Not ever."

I look up, confused. "Why?"

"You don't remember the stories I told you? Of what lives out there?" She begins to pace. "Dragons and demons twisted by madness. Witches who steal the breath of girls like you. Monster shifters who can no longer return to their skin. There are things that would rip you apart."

"But Mother, I just want to see how the grass feels beneath my feet or how it feels to take a dip in the lake. I won't go far…"

Mother doesn't blink. "You want to leave the tower?" She says it like I've just asked if I can jump into a fire.

I nod, though my palms are suddenly damp. "Just to the lake, no farther."

She presses her lips together and walks slowly to the window. She looks out, her fingers curling around the sill. "You don't know what's out there, Roxy."

"I know there are trees, flowers, and animals. I know there's water. I can see, Mother!"

She turns to face me. "And you think that's all there is? Trees, water, soft moss, and pretty birds? No, love. That's just what the forest *wants* you to see."

I frown. "What does that mean?"

"There are monsters in that forest," she says, matter-of-factly. "Real ones. They crawl through the underbrush when the sun goes down. Some walk on two legs, some on four. Some fly, if you can believe it. And they love sweet girls who've never seen a single shadow past their windowsill."

My chest tightens, but I lift my chin. "You've never said anything like this before."

"You were a child before," she snaps then softens. "Now you're almost grown, and almost grown means curious, which means dangerous."

I cross my arms. "I am grown!" I shout.

She doesn't hesitate.

"There are bonehounds. Starving, half-dead things with skin stretched tight over broken skeletons. They smell blood and chase it for miles. There are *whisperers*, creatures that climb inside your head and convince you to walk off cliffs or drink poison. There's a woman made of smoke who turns into a bird and pecks out eyes with her beak. A man with bark for skin who collects girls and grows them into his tree."

"That's not real."

She walks to me, calm and slow, and cups my cheek in her hand. "It's real. And I've kept you safe from it all. Every year, girls go missing from nearby villages. The monsters come down at night and take them. I've seen the claw marks myself."

I shake my head. "Then why do you go out there?"

"Because I know where *not* to step. I know the signs. I can feel the air when it changes." Her eyes narrow. "You can't. And if you leave this tower—even for a minute—you'll never make it back." Her voice is low, certain.

"And the witches?" I ask, quieter now.

She leans closer. "The worst of all. Some say they live forever. That they keep snakes for husbands and rats for spies. That they steal children and trap souls in mirrors."

I swallow hard.

Her voice is sharp. "I've protected you. Hidden you. And this tower? It's the only place you're truly safe. It's not a prison, Roxy. It's a fortress."

I glance around. "It doesn't feel like one."

Her gaze grows distant for a moment, then she pats my cheek and steps back. "You're not well. That's why all this talk is bubbling up."

"I'm just—restless."

"You're overheated and anxious. That's what comes from being too clever for your own good." She reaches for her pouch and pulls out a sprig of something dry and sharp-smelling. "I'll fetch stronger herbs. Ones that will calm this… fever in you."

"When?"

"I'll leave now. I may be gone for a while. A few weeks, perhaps. Take your medicine now, dear."

My stomach sinks, but I nod. "All right." I put the bitter herbs on my tongue and swallow.

She walks toward the window then pauses. "Promise me you won't leave."

I nod again. "I promise."

I throw my braid out the window, and it tumbles to the ground. Mother climbs down my hair, and I watch her fade into the horizon.

My mind drifts. I picture myself stepping out of the tower, my bare feet touching the soft moss, the grass cool and wet between my toes. Freedom, just for a moment, tastes sweeter than anything I've known.

I imagine the cool lake water slipping over my bare skin. The way the sunlight would scatter across the surface, turning every ripple to sparkling glass. I can almost hear the soft lap of waves against the shore, smell the damp earth and hibiscus that grow thick at the water's edge.

But then Mother's words creep in.

Monsters with teeth like knives, eyes that never blink, breathing slow and silent in the darkness.

I wonder if they stalk so carefully that I'd never hear them coming. Would I know they were there before they tore into me? Or is it all just a story? A story to keep me trapped inside these cold stone walls....

I glance around the tower—my whole world—and it feels smaller than ever. But outside? Outside is unknown. It calls to me like a distant song I don't quite remember, a melody tangled up with my own heartbeat. The ache in my chest grows sharper, more urgent.

Even though Mother's warnings echo in my mind, a small ember of hope flickers stubbornly inside me. The tower might be tall and sealed tight, but no walls, no matter how thick, can cage a heart determined to be free. I remind myself that this place can't hold me forever. One day, somehow, I will find a way out.

I think about the stories I've woven in my mind over the years, the tales I've sung softly to myself when the loneliness crept too close. Stories of brave girls who climbed beyond their prison towers, who slipped past monsters and witches and found the sun waiting just for them. Those girls don't stay trapped forever. Neither will I.

I imagine the first step, feeling the soft earth beneath my bare feet, cold, rough, and real. I imagine running through the trees, the sun warming my face, the scent of pine and wildflowers thick in the air.

I imagine hearing the laughter of others, voices calling my name, from a place full of light and life.

THE POISON IN THE JAR

Leo

I wake to the hush of dawn and the cool damp of dew clinging to my fur.

For a moment, I can't recall where I am.

Then I see the valley stretched around me, lush and unreal. The tower shines quiet and unmoving in the pale gold of early morning. The wind here carries no scent of danger, only water lilies, damp moss, and that same strange sweetness. Lavender and honey.

My ears twitch.

A rustle, soft but certain, stirs the ferns nearby. I lift my head, my nose twitching, senses sharpening.

A woman steps into the clearing. She's tall and thin, wrapped in a dark green cloak that brushes the grass as she moves. Her presence feels... sinister. I can smell the wolfsbane in her pouch.

She's barefoot but walks like she owns the earth beneath her, and I crouch lower behind a bramble, barely daring to breathe.

She stops below the tower and lifts her head.

"Let down your hair," she calls, her voice melodic and strange, tinged with a lilt I can't place.

There's a moment of silence.

Then, impossibly, something unspools from the open window high above.

Hair.

Golden, thick, and gleaming like sunlight itself. A braid, tighter and longer than any rope I've ever seen, unfurls from the window and tumbles down the tower's smooth stone face.

I stare, stunned.

The woman doesn't hesitate. She gathers the braid in both hands, tests its strength with a quick tug, then begins to climb.

Not rope. Not vines. Hair.

Whoever the girl is up there, I can't see her face—only the gleam of her braid, catching the light in soft gold.

The woman ascends swiftly, hand over hand, her feet braced against the tower like she's done it a hundred times. I watch, half in awe, half in disbelief. No door. No stairs. Only this—this bizarre, beautiful method of entrance. She disappears through the window, vanishing into the dark within.

I move slightly, my paws quiet against the moss. I don't move closer, not yet. The air is too still. The tower is too quiet.

Who is the girl? A prisoner? A witch?

And the woman—mother, mentor, captor?

Minutes pass. Birds stir in the trees again. The sky brightens.

Then—movement.

The braid unfurls again, and the woman reappears, sliding down the golden rope with practiced ease. This time, she carries a basket tucked under one arm, lands light on her feet, and brushes her palms clean.

I expect her to look around, but she doesn't. She doesn't seem aware she's being watched.

With the basket balanced on her hip, she turns and walks back into the trees, toward the wall of vines I passed through last night.

I don't follow. Not yet.

Instead, I stare up at the window as the braid disappears.

I tuck my muzzle between my paws and wait, my ears still tuned to every sound. The moment the woman disappears through the vine curtain, I finally exhale.

Still hidden in the undergrowth, I lift my head and stare again at the tower.

Who is she?

I take a breath and shift.

It's slower this time, deliberate. My wolf recedes, leaving behind skin, muscle, and bone, and I crouch low in the bushes, naked and cold in the damp morning air. My heart pounds harder now—not from fear, but from something else. Anticipation, maybe. Curiosity. That strange ache that started last night and hasn't let go since.

I wait a few more minutes, just to be sure the tall woman in green is truly gone.

Then, I rise slightly, brushing leaves from my arms, and glance up at the window again. The braid is gone now, reeled back up inside. I can't see anyone, but I know she's there. Watching, maybe. Listening.

I clear my throat softly. "Miss?" I call, trying not to shout. My voice sounds rough after so long in wolf form. "Miss, are you there?"

A few heartbeats pass. Then a shape appears at the arched window, tentative and cautious. And then she steps fully into view.

My breath catches.

She's the most beautiful woman I've ever seen.

Not just pretty. Not just striking. *Otherworldly.*

Her delicate features catch the morning light just right—full lips, a straight nose, and wide eyes that hold a mixture of curiosity and concern.

Her gaze sweeps the clearing below. I duck slightly behind the bush, raising a hand in cautious greeting.

"Hi," I call, keeping my voice low and non-threatening. "Sorry to bother you. I'm... not dangerous. I promise."

She tilts her head slightly, still searching for the source of my voice.

"I'm down here," I add. "Behind the bushes. Just... give me a second." I make sure she can't see me and call up again. "I, uh—this is awkward, but I was in a fight, and I lost my clothes." I wince at how that sounds. "Could you possibly toss me down something? A blanket, maybe? Or anything. Just something I can put on."

She doesn't answer right away, and for a long moment, I think she may have disappeared for good.

But then she leans a little closer to the window, peering through the branches.

Her voice floats down, soft and melodic. "A fight?"

"Yeah. With bandits," I say quickly. "It's a long story, but I promise I'm not here to hurt you or anyone. I got separated from my group and found this place by accident. I'll leave if you want me to, just... preferably not naked."

Her lips twitch. I think she's trying not to smile.

"I could find something," she says slowly. "But you have to stay there. No climbing. No tricks."

"Of course," I say. "No climbing. No tricks. Just desperate for pants."

She leaves the window. I sag with relief and lean back on the tower.

A part of me still can't believe this is happening. The tower, the braid, the enchanted valley, and now her. It all feels like a dream I'm afraid to wake from. But the cold air and scratchy leaves say otherwise.

A moment later, a pair of pants and a top flutter down from the window. They're clearly several sizes too small, but I wrestle myself into them anyway. Once I'm dressed, I finally notice the tiny flower pattern stitched along the hem—and the ruffled sleeves.

Fantastic. I probably look like a deranged garden gnome.

When I'm done, I step out just slightly—not too far, not too bold. I glance back up at the window.

"Thank you," I say.

She's already gone again, but I know she's still listening, and now, I'm certain of one thing: I have to know her name.

I take a cautious step closer, no longer needing to hide now that

I'm dressed in the clothes she dropped. "Miss?" I call softly, gazing up toward the stone arch.

There's a rustle, and then her face appears once more, her golden hair spilling around her shoulders like sunlight poured into human form.

"Are you still here?" she asks in a feather-light voice.

"Still here," I reply. "And still very thankful for the clothes."

She looks down and bursts into laughter at the sight of me.

I give her a moment to catch her breath.

"Thank you. I don't recall how long it's been since I laughed so hard," she says.

"You're very welcome. I didn't get your name," I ask, stepping a little closer. "I'd like to know it… if that's all right."

A long pause.

Then: "Roxanna," she says. "But my mother calls me Roxy."

Roxy. It suits her—unexpected, bright, warm. It rolls through my mind like the name of someone I might already know.

"I'm Leo," I say. "From Moon River."

She tilts her head, frowning slightly. "I don't know where that is."

"It's not far," I say. "A few peaks and valleys over." I clear my throat and summon all the courage I have. "Roxy, I know this probably sounds strange, but may I come up? And before you say no—consider this: I'm standing here dressed like a fairy princess. No one wearing ruffles and flowers can do anyone any harm, right?"

The golden braid unfurls once more from the window like spun sunlight tumbling from the sky. It sways gently in the wind, impossibly long, impossibly strong.

I hesitate only a second before gripping it with both hands.

The climb is harder than I expected. The braid holds, thick and tightly woven, but my arms burn halfway up. Still, I climb. My bare feet scrape the smooth stone, fingers tightening on every twist of hair until I reach the window ledge.

She steps back to make room as I swing one leg over the sill and then the other. I drop lightly into the tower room.

It's small but beautiful. Stone walls polished smooth by time, a small hearth cold in the corner, dried herbs and flowers hanging from the beams. A basin, a low table, stacks of folded linen, and a neatly made bed. Everything smells like peaches, lavender, and lemon balm. Like comfort and peace.

She stands by the wall with her arms crossed loosely, eyes wary but not unkind.

"Thank you," I say, breathing hard from the climb. "For trusting me."

She gives a small nod. "You weren't supposed to find this place."

"I figured," I say, stepping just inside. "But now that I have..."

She sways suddenly, her hand reaching for the wall. Her expression tightens—pain, confusion.

"Roxy?" I say, stepping forward instinctively. "What's wrong?"

"I—" She takes a deep breath then staggers.

I catch her before she hits the floor.

Her body is cold, and she's gone pale with her lips parted slightly as her head rests against my chest. Her braid spills around us like a golden rope. She's unconscious, but still breathing.

My heart pounds.

Whatever enchantment lives in this valley, whatever secrets this tower holds, I've just walked straight into the middle of it.

And now Roxy has collapsed in my arms.

I kneel slowly, cradling her gently as I lower her to the rug. "Hey," I whisper. "Roxy, can you hear me?"

No response.

I brush the hair from her face.

What the hell is going on here, and how do I help her?

I lay her gently on the rug. Her skin is clammy, her breathing shallow but steady. I stay there a moment, kneeling beside her, unsure if I should call for help—though I don't even know *who* I'd call. She and the woman with the basket seem to be the only ones who live here. If this valley really is enchanted, if this tower is somehow... hidden... then help might be impossible to summon.

"Roxy," I whisper. "Wake up."

She doesn't stir.

I let out a breath and slowly rise. The room is warmer now than I'd expected, and it smells like dried flowers and something deadly: wolfsbane.

I don't mean to snoop, but I have to make sure she's not hurt, or at least figure out *what* might've caused her to faint.

I walk carefully to the shelves along the wall. There are jars of dried herbs, hand-labeled in delicate script: valerian, yarrow, motherwort, wolfsbane—

I pause, noticing that one's corked tighter than the rest.

My gaze settles on Roxy—she's a shifter, I can tell without a doubt. There's no blood, no bruises, no sign she fought back. She's lying there as though she's been mildly poisoned. It has to be the bane.

I should run away as fast as I can and never look back. Nothing good can come from trying to help her, and yet, I'm drawn to her. Roxy is beautiful, but this is not just attraction. It's something deeper. A tug in my chest, in my *bones.* Like I'm not just pulled to her—I'm *bound* to her.

But why?

I look back at the wolfsbane in the jar next to the other herbs, barely noticing the faintest shift of movement. The brush of fabric. The creak of a floorboard that had stayed silent until now.

I turn—too late.

She's already on me.

The broom handle slams into the backs of my knees with enough force to buckle them. I go down hard, the rug doing nothing to soften the blow. Pain shoots through my skull a second later as it cracks against stone.

Everything goes black.

THE WOLF IN THE MAN

Roxy

HE'S NOT MOVING.

I stand over him with the broom handle clutched tight in both hands, the end still vibrating faintly from the force of the blow. He went down hard—his legs knocked clean out from under him, head smacking against the stone floor with a dull thud.

And now he's lying there, sprawled out like a rag doll.

Wearing my flowered pajamas.

The sight would be funny if I weren't still shaking. My sleeves, the ones with the ruffled cuffs, are stretched absurdly tight over his muscular forearms. The tiny embroidered daisies at the hem of the shirt ride up his abdominal muscles, which I can't help but allow my eyes to linger over. And the pants, well… they only go about halfway down his calves.

He looks absolutely ridiculous, and somehow, impossibly hand-some. I stand over him, studying his face. Dark hair, a strong jaw, lips with the hint of a smirk even while unconscious. I've never seen a man before, but if I had to guess... he must be one of the better-looking ones.

I grab the sheet off my bed and begin wrapping it tightly around him so he can't move and attack me when he awakes.

It feels surreal. Tying up a stranger. A *man*. A *real man*. Not just some blurry idea from one of Mother's warnings or a painted figure in an old storybook.

There's a small scrape on his temple where he hit the floor—nothing too serious, I hope. I don't want him dead. I just want to know who he is, what he's doing here, and how he found *me*. Luring him up here was the only way I could find out if others know where I am–like the monsters Mother is always warning me about. If he could find me, they could find me–right?

"Why is he so comfortable wearing a floral top with ruffles?" I laugh under my breath as I knot the last tie. "Serves him right." I step back and fold my arms. The room is quiet now except for the faint ticking of the clock on the mantle and the wind brushing gently against the tower window.

I drag a stool across the floor and plant it a safe distance away, still far enough that if he lunges, he won't reach me. I sit, broom still in hand, my knuckles tight around the handle. I've never tied anyone up before, but I think I've done a decent job. I don't want to hurt him. I just need answers.

Because people don't just wander into this valley. No one's supposed to know where the tower is. There's no path, no signs, no way to cross the wild terrain without getting hopelessly lost.

And yet... here he is. Did he follow Mother? Was he sent?

My thoughts swirl, darting from one possibility to the next. I study his face again, trying to find answers in the shape of his brow or the slope of his cheekbone. Nothing. He looks... peaceful, almost. Which is a strange thing to say about someone bound hand and foot on my floor.

Maybe when he wakes up, he'll explain himself. Maybe he'll say something clever, or maybe he'll scream, and thrash, and demand to be released. Either way, I'll be ready.

I glance at the teapot on the hearth. Maybe I should make some tea. For me. Not him.

Definitely *not* for him.

Though… if he's going to be tied up for a while, I suppose it would be polite.

His eyelids twitch first.

I grip the broom handle tighter and scoot forward, alert. One eye opens then the other. He squints at the light coming through the window, blinks a few times, then tries to sit up, only to find himself completely bound.

His head flops back to the floor with a groan.

"You're awake," I say, keeping my voice steady. "Good."

He turns his head toward me slowly. "Did I lose a fight?"

I don't respond. He already knows the answer, his wrists tugging against the sheet bindings as he tests them, but he's not going anywhere.

"Who are you?" I demand. "Why were you sneaking around my tower?"

He winces. "Can we start with 'Hello'? Or 'Are you all right'? I think I might've cracked my skull on your floor."

"We introduced ourselves, and next thing I know, I'm waking up," I shout. "What happened to me? And how did you even find this valley?"

He exhales and moves as much as his restraints allow. "I got lost in a storm and found the valley. Before too long, I stumbled upon your tower. I didn't even know this place existed. At first, I thought it might be abandoned or enchanted."

My stomach turns. I ignore it.

He goes on, "When I saw you—I didn't even *see* you properly—I just saw your hair, and I got curious. Honest. I swear I wasn't trying to steal anything, or hurt you, or whatever you're imagining with that very intense stare of yours."

I open my mouth to respond, but the room tilts.

My vision blurs at the edges. The broom slips from my grip and clatters to the floor. I gasp and double over, clutching my stomach.

"Hey," he says, voice sharp now. "Are you okay?"

My breath comes fast and shallow. My head pounds. My skin burns. I crawl to the shelf near the hearth and grope blindly for the tiny jar of crushed leaves, green and silver, nestled beside the dried herbs and salves. My fingers close around it.

"No, don't—" Leo says. "Wait, *don't* take *that!*"

I ignore him. I uncork the jar and press the leaves to my tongue, swallowing it down with a shaking hand.

The pain spikes instantly.

Heat floods my chest. My throat tightens, eyes blurring with tears. I fall onto my side, convulsing slightly as the world tips again, harder this time.

"*Roxy!*" he shouts, struggling against the knots. "That was wolfs-bane—you can't—why would you—"

"I have to," I whisper. "It'll make me better."

"No, it's *poisoning* you," he growls, straining against the sheets like he could break them just by will alone. "Who told you to take that? Why would you ever…. Dammit, untie me!"

The pain is like fire now, clawing through my insides. I curl into a tighter ball, sobbing through gritted teeth.

He's still shouting, still yanking at the knots, but I can't make sense of the words. My ears are ringing. My thoughts are coming undone.

Everything inside me screams to get out. My skin feels too tight. My bones feel like they're trying to move beneath me. I clutch my stomach and gasp again.

I don't know how long it lasts—seconds? Hours?

Then, gradually, the pain begins to dull. Not vanish, just fade enough that I can open my eyes again. I'm soaked in sweat. Shaking. Dizzy. Alive, somehow.

When I lift my head, Leo is still tied up—but he's stopped shouting. His jaw is clenched tight, his brow furrowed in a way that looks more like worry than rage.

"I told you not to take it," he says.

My body shudders once then stills. I can breathe again. I blink up at the ceiling beams, my heart still hammering in my ears, and feel sweat cooling on my skin. I struggle to sit up.

"Roxy," Leo says, his voice gentler now. "Please. Let me help you."

I turn my head toward him. He's still ridiculous-looking in my too-small, flower-trimmed clothes. His expression doesn't match the outfit. He looks concerned and serious. No trace of laughter or trickery.

"I don't even know you," I rasp.

He nods. "You're right, you don't know me. But I do know what's happening to you."

I roll my eyes. "No, you don't. How could you?"

He shakes his head. "That wasn't a reaction to an illness you just experienced. It was a reaction to the medicine. Your body was fighting it off. I know, and the reason I know is because you're like me."

My stomach clenches—not with pain this time, but something worse. Dread. "Like you?"

"A shifter," he says softly. "You're not human. Not fully. I knew the second I saw you, and the medicine is called *wolfsbane*—your body is rejecting it because it's poison to our kind."

"That's not true," I whisper. "My mother... she said—"

"She lied," he interrupts. "I don't know why, but she did. Or someone lied to her. But I swear on my life, Roxy, you're a wolf shifter. Same as me."

I stare at him. It's absurd. All of it. And yet...

Somewhere, deep inside, something pulses at the sound of that word.

Wolf.

"I—I don't believe you."

"I'll prove it," he says. "Untie me, and I'll leave, but when I do, watch me. I'll shift as I run. You'll see it with your own eyes."

My hands tremble in my lap. "And then you'll be gone?"

He hesitates. "Only if you want me to be."

I look at him, tied up and earnest, his hair mussed. A man I've never seen before today. And yet, after speaking with him for only a few moments, I don't want him to go.

"Would you come back?" I whisper.

His eyes soften. "If you asked me to."

I chew my lip, my whole body still weak and aching. "Come back tonight."

He smiles, lopsided and genuine. "I will."

It takes every ounce of strength I have to crawl toward him. My arms feel like overcooked noodles, but I manage to work the knots loose. The moment his hands are free, he rubs his wrists and immediately reaches toward me—but stops just short of touching.

"Thank you," he says.

I nod, unsure if I should thank him, too.

He gets to his feet and glances toward the window.

"I will see you again?" I ask quietly.

He nods. "I give you my word."

I grab my braid and carefully lower it down the side of the tower again, the familiar routine made heavier by everything I've just learned.

Leo climbs down, his bare feet finding the stones with surprising ease. Just before he drops down the last few feet, he looks up at me and says, "Don't take the wolfsbane again. Promise me."

"I—" I hesitate. "I give you my word."

And then he drops. I lean out the window, my heart thudding as he hits the grass below and starts to run—barefoot, long-legged and fast.

He's barely ten paces away when it happens.

Right before my eyes, his body ripples like heat on stone. Fur bursts from his skin. His limbs bend and shift, and then he's gone.

In his place is a wolf—huge, sleek, and dark as night, racing toward the trees like a shadow.

I clutch the windowsill, my breath catching in my throat.

He wasn't lying.

And now I've asked him to come back.

There's no denying what I just saw.

I might not know the word *shifter*, might never have heard it spoken until today, but I know what I saw was real. No trick of the eye. No fairy tale. One moment, he was a man—and the next, a wolf, swift, wild, and impossibly fast, vanishing into the trees below.

He *is* what he says he is.

But me? I shake my head slowly, my fingers still curled around the window ledge. No. I can't be. I've lived my whole life up here in this tower, and I've never felt anything close to what he described. Never felt claws in my skin or fur beneath it. Never howled at the moon or hungered for raw meat or whatever it is wolves do. I'm not like him. I *can't* be.

And yet… something in my bones hums with a strange awareness. A soft, restless stirring I've never felt before tonight.

I press my forehead to the stone frame of the window, pulling my braid back inside.

I should be afraid, and maybe I *am*, a little. But mostly, I'm… curious.

Who is this man who climbed my braid and broke into my solitude? The man who told me things I'm not sure I want to know—and yet, I can't stop turning them over in my mind?

And why, after all he said, am I already looking forward to seeing him again?

THE PUP IN THE LEGEND

Leo

THE FOREST RUSHES PAST IN SHADES OF GREEN, THE SUNLIGHT CUTTING through the canopy in slivers. My paws drum the ground in a steady rhythm, swift, sure, and quiet. Every inch of me hums with strength and purpose, but my thoughts drift, caught somewhere between instincts and wonder.

Roxy.

Her name tugs at me like a thorn caught in my fur. I didn't expect to meet her. Not in a place like that, and not tucked away in some forgotten tower like a magic spell gone sideways. I sure as hell didn't expect to care, but I do.

I slow my pace near a small hollow, circling once, then drop to the ground and roll deep in the grass, twisting until the scent of earth and moss clings to my coat. I leave it thick, pungent—*mine*. A breadcrumb trail of crushed grass, scent, fur, and wild magic. I don't want to forget how to get back. I *can't* forget.

Her scent is still in my nose—lavender, woodsmoke, fear, and something else. Something old and unclaimed. The kind of scent that changes when a young shifter recognizes their pack, their first bond. She has no one. No Alpha. No tether. No clue.

But she's one of us. I'm sure of it.

I break into a run again, faster now, threading between the trees. I make deliberate paw prints in the mud near a creek bed. I double back and run the stretch again, just to deepen the impressions.

The leaves are damp underfoot, the sun overhead. I stop again near a low ridge and press my side into the brush, twisting to leave my musk on the bark. Another marker. Another sign for myself—*remember this place*.

My heart beats a little faster thinking of her at the window. Gorgeous eyes, soft lips, and the longest braid anyone has ever grown.

It's not just curiosity that pulls my thoughts toward her. It's not just the shock of finding someone like me, but hidden, strange, powerful without knowing. It's *her*. That fire behind her fear.

I slow again to cross a narrow stretch of rocky slope. I step deliberately, leaving dust and loose stones scattered in my wake. Another sign. Another memory.

I'll be back.

I swore it, and I will.

The scent of my pack reaches me before I see them. I lurch up the final incline and spot the mouth of the cave, low and narrow, ringed with tangled roots.

"Alpha Leo?" comes a voice through the mind-link. It's Zekia.

I stop to catch my breath. *"It's me."*

"Finally," Tarin growls. *"We were about to assume you either got distracted chasing a squirrel or died."*

"Funny. No, but I did find something."

"Food?" Briar asks, hopeful.

"No," I say. *"Something... someone."*

They all go still.

I glance back out at the trees, the trail I left behind. *"There's a girl in a tower, and she's a wolf shifter. She doesn't know it yet, but she is. She's been up there her whole life, I think. Hidden. Alone."*

"You're sure she's a wolf shifter?" Briar asks.

I nod. *"I saw it. Felt it. She's like us."*

Silence hangs thick in the cave.

Finally, Tarin mutters, *"Then I guess you're going back."*

"Tonight." And in my chest, something ancient and restless stirs. *"She didn't know what wolfsbane is. She doesn't know she's a wolf shifter."*

"Did she take some?" Briar asks.

"Yes, her mother has been giving it to her. I don't know the full story yet, but I think she has her locked up in the tower..." I trail off.

There's a shared pulse of silence in the link. Not doubt—*worry.* Zekia finally exhales through his nose. *"If someone hid her away, there's a chance this could mean trouble."*

"I know, but I can't ignore my instincts. She asked me to return. She's not a threat. She's just... alone. Now, let's get home before the others send out a search party for our search party."

The sun's high by the time we make it back to Moon River. The forest thins, and the scent of wolf fills the air long before we reach the outer ridge. Familiar paths curve beneath our feet, worn smooth from generations of patrols. In the distance, wooden watchtowers rise from the hills.

As we crest the final ridge, the central clearing opens before us, stone houses, smoke curling from chimneys, voices carrying on the breeze.

And there, waiting at the edge of the training ring, stands Marek. A cloak lies across his arms, his stance rigid as always. He looks like a statue carved from iron.

"Where the hell have you four been?" he asks, his voice low but sharp.

I shift, and Marek wraps the cloak around me as I rise. "Storm caught us outside the mind-link range. We took shelter but got split up for a while."

He narrows his eyes. "You look like you've been crawling beneath the roots."

"I haven't," I admit. "but I found the secret Moonbeam Valley, and I met someone."

Briar steps forward beside me, still in wolf form. *"She's one of us, Marek."*

"Who is she? Is she a rogue?" Marek asks, his eyes widening.

As the others on the search team return to their homes to shift, I tell Marek all I know about Roxy.

"She's hidden deep in Moonbeam Valley in a tower. She had long golden hair. She's beautiful… but she's a wolf shifter with no pack, no training. She doesn't even know she's like us."

Marek exhales slowly, pinching the bridge of his nose. "And you told her?"

"I had to," I say. "She was dying. She was taking wolfsbane. She thinks it's medicine."

Marek laughs. "She sounds like the Golden Elm Princess, from the story."

I stop walking. *"Who?"*

His eyes are full of laughter as they move to mine. "The girl in the legend. The one we weren't supposed to talk about when we were pups."

I frown. "What legend?"

Marek leans back, his expression unreadable. "I guess you never heard of it? Well, we weren't supposed to speak of it. You're sure you've never heard it?"

I step closer. "Tell me the story!"

"About twenty years ago, the Luna of the Golden Elm pack was pregnant with her first child. The whole territory was holding its breath as she and the Alpha had been trying for some time. Then she started getting sick. Nothing dangerous at first. She said she needed a tea, one with chamomile, clover, ginger, and something else. Something she couldn't name."

I narrow my eyes. "None of those ingredients are that strange."

"No," Marek agrees. "But this Luna knew what her baby needed and what would make her feel better. She said she could *taste* the missing part. Said she'd know it when she smelled it. They tried everything. Dozens of blends. Nothing satisfied her. She was wasting away."

I stay silent, listening.

"One night, the Alpha went out hunting and tracked a wounded stag deep into the eastern woods—farther than he'd ever patrolled. That's when he found a secret garden, hidden in a sunken glen. Not wild, but planted and tended. He said there were rows of herbs, vines, and fruit trees bent low with peaches and lemons. In the center, he saw a bush covered in blossoms. Pale white flowers, tipped with light purple."

My heart lurches. "Rapunzel flowers."

Marek nods once. "Camoanula Rapunculus. Also known as the Rapunzel flower. He plucked a handful, and the moment he did, the bush withered. It just died right there. It startled him, so he ran. He brought the flowers home and ground them into his Luna's tea."

"And it worked?"

"Better than anything ever had. She drank it once, and the illness stopped. Her strength returned. Her pregnancy stabilized. When the pup was born, she had the thickest hair anyone had ever seen—long, golden-blonde, with streaks of red like firelight."

I swallow hard.

Roxy.

"She grew fast, healthy and strong, but one night when she was nine months old, a coven of displaced witches from all over the territories of Vaeloria and Hexeton, broke into the Alpha and Luna's bedroom. They weren't old, twisted, or ugly witches. They were young, beautiful, sharp eyed, and cold. They told the Alpha he had stolen from them. That he had taken what didn't belong to him."

"The Rapunzel flowers," I murmur.

Marek nods again. "They said the flowers were tied to life and youth and that taking them would unravel the threads of fate. The witches showed the Alpha and Luna of Golden Elm visions of what would happen if they didn't give the baby girl over. The visions were horrible."

My breath catches in my chest. "What did the visions show?"

"The visions showed their entire pack lifeless. Women, children, pups, including theirs. The witches said they would kill them all but that if they surrendered the child, their pack could live."

"They didn't believe them, did they?"

"Not at first," Marek responds. "But then the witches told them to look out the window of their castle. The castle courtyard was littered in corpses. The witches had already killed everyone in the courtyard. While the Luna clutched the baby tightly, the Alpha rushed down to the courtyard and through the village. Everyone was dead. The evil witches said if they gave them the baby, they would give everyone in the pack their lives back."

"What did they do?" I ask, heart sinking.

"He gave the child to them."

I stare at him, fists clenched.

Marek continues, "The Alpha made the hardest choice a father can make. He handed his newborn daughter to witches because he believed it would save her and his pack."

"Did it?"

Marek nods his head slowly. "The people weren't really dead. It was some sort of sleeping spell. The witches left, and they woke up, but as for the girl, we don't know. The witches vanished with the baby. No trace."

I think of Roxy's eyes, and the way she *felt* familiar before I ever knew her name.

"You think she's the girl?" I whisper.

"I don't know what I think," Marek says. "But if the witches kept her hidden all these years, if she grew up never knowing what she was... that tower of yours might have something to do with it."

I let the silence stretch. Finally, I say, "I'm going back."

"I figured," Marek replies. "Just be ready, Leo. If that witch coven is still out there—if they hid the girl for a reason—they won't give her up without a fight."

"I always figured I just didn't have a mate," I say quietly. "Most wolves do. I thought maybe I just... was one of the unlucky ones."

Marek doesn't respond right away. Just crosses his arms and waits for more.

"I wasn't *waiting* for someone," I go on. "I wasn't holding out hope. I made peace with it a long time ago." I shake my head. "But Roxy— she's different. I feel it. In my gut. In my bones. It's like gravity."

Marek lets out a slow breath, nodding. "You're pulled to her."

"More than pulled." I pause. "She feels like she's *mine*. And I don't even know her."

"That happens," Marek says. "Fate doesn't follow rules. But Leo—"

"I know," I cut in. "I'll be careful."

He steps forward and grips my shoulder. "She might be your mate, but she could also be the center of a legend. If witches raised her, there could be more at play than instinct. So yes—follow the pull. Trust it. But keep your eyes open."

"I will."

Marek nods once then releases me. "Go get her, but don't lose yourself doing it."

That evening, as the sun dips low and shadows lengthen across the pines, I pack a satchel in silence: clothes, a hunting knife, and jerky wrapped tight in cloth. It's not much, but I need to travel light and fast.

Marek watches without comment until I tie the flap closed.

"Sure you want to do this tonight?" he asks finally.

"I left a clear trail for myself," I tell him. "The longer I wait, the colder it gets. The wind could carry the scent off by morning."

He doesn't argue. He just steps forward and grips my shoulder. "You come back with her, Leo."

I nod.

We walk out to the edge of the tree line. I strip down, pack my clothes, and shift.

It's a fast, clean change. The bones snap, fur blooms down my arms and spine. My paws touch the dirt as my senses sharpen all at once. I shake, getting used to the weight again.

Marek doesn't flinch as he steps behind me and tightens the straps around my body. The satchel rests flat between my shoulders, cinched snugly so it won't slide when I run.

"You sure it's balanced?" I ask through the mind-link.

He gives it a tug. "Won't move. Good luck, Alpha."

I bare my teeth in thanks then bolt.

The world blurs. Trees whip past in smears of green and brown, the ground soft beneath my paws. I don't slow. I don't need to. My trail is there, just as I left it. A line of paw prints through soft loam. A broken fern. A brush of flattened grass. And the scent.

My scent.

Each time I come across one of the places I rolled, on purpose, I pause and breathe deep. That earthy, slightly sharp musk is *mine*, and it draws me like a thread. Through the gully, across the stones slick with moss, past the creek.

The night grows cooler as I ascend into the higher woods again. Stars break through the clouds above, faint but enough to see by. I don't need them. My nose and instincts lead me, unwavering. A fox scurries away as I charge past. An owl hoots above, wings brushing low over the trees. Every step draws me closer to her.

Then, all at once, the vines are before me, beckoning me into the secret valley once again.

Moonbeam Valley glows under the moonlight. The grass rustles gently, and Roxy's tower stands tall and silent. My heart pounds hard in my chest. I slow, creeping to the edge of the clearing.

She's not in the window, but she's here. I can *feel* her. I lower myself into the tall grass, my ears alert, every muscle thrumming.

This time, I'm not leaving without her.

THE ROOM IN THE INN

Roxy

The stone walls press in colder than usual tonight, though the fire crackles in the hearth, and the candles still burn steady and bright. I stand at the window, my eyes fixed on the tree line, willing Leo to return like he said he would. Moonlight spills across the woods, painting everything in silver, and I search the shadows, my heart tight with hope.

He said he'd come back tonight. He promised, like it was something sacred. And part of me, against all reason, believes him.

But the other part? The one that's lived in this tower for nearly twenty-one years? That part keeps whispering that I'll never see him again. That he's like every other dream I've dared to have: beautiful, and yet, always impossible.

He said I was a wolf. A *shifter*, like him.

The word still sits strange on my tongue. It sounds like a story, something from Mother's bedtime tales, not something real.

Could it be true? Could I really be one of them?

It doesn't feel true. I've never shifted. Never even felt anything close. No claws, no snarling, no hunger for hunting or howling at the moon.

And yet...

I close my eyes, and I see Leo. This morning when he ran through the valley, a black wolf, I should've been terrified. I wasn't. I was mesmerized. He was majestic, graceful, and fierce. It only made me want to see him again even more.

I don't know why I trust him. I shouldn't. He could be lying, and he most definitely could be dangerous.

Yet, I do trust him. I trust him in a way I can't explain, like I've known him my whole life.

When he asked me to promise not to take the wolfsbane, I didn't hesitate. Even though I still don't understand what it does. Mother insists I take it every time I feel ill, but Leo sounded so sure when he said it would hurt me.

The leaves rustle softly in the wind, and I wonder what it would be like to *touch* the world instead of just watching it from the window. To feel the earth give beneath my bare feet, instead of solid stone. To run without walls. To dive into the lake that winks at me through the trees.

And people. *Any* people. Not just Mother. My world begins and ends in this tower. I've never been at a dinner table full of family and friends. I've never had a friend....

My twenty-first birthday is soon, and I don't want another quiet dinner with my mother, the same song she sings every year, the same solitary candle on the same rose-petal cupcake. I want noise, laughter, and new faces. I want to *live*.

But—

I CLOSE MY EYES AGAIN. I'M ALL SHE HAS.

I remember her face when I told her I didn't want to stay in this tower forever and that I wanted to leave. She warned me never to even think of such things....

And what if I'm wrong? What if I leave, and it breaks her? What if

I'm chasing a life that ends up hurting the only person who's ever loved me?

The doubt coils in my stomach. Maybe the tower *is* where I belong.

A shadow flashes at the edge of the trees, and suddenly, I can't catch my breath.

I see a blur of movement, black fur shining in the moonlight. Leo's wolf makes powerful strides, his eyes bright with purpose.

I leap away from the window, my pulse pounding. Rushing to the mirror, my fingers shake as I smooth my hair, pinch color into my cheeks, and tug the sleeves of my gown into place.

Maybe he's here to change everything.

A few moments pass in silence, the kind that stretches and fizzes with anticipation.

Then I hear it.

"Roxy," Leo's voice calls from below, low, and warm, "are you up there?"

I nearly knock over the candle scrambling to the window. "Yes! I'm here!"

"Could I come up, please?" he asks.

"Look out below!" I call back, grabbing my braid and flinging it over the sill.

A few moments later, he's swinging one leg over the ledge and stepping into the tower with a grin.

"Nice to see you again," he says, brushing pine needles from his dark hair.

"I wasn't sure you'd come back."

He arches a brow. "You doubted me?"

"A little."

He shrugs, as if he expected that. "Well, I *did* have to outrun a very angry raccoon to get here. But I said I'd come, didn't I?"

"You did," I say, letting a smile tug at my lips.

I glance at him properly now. His tall boots are stitched with gold thread, his trousers look like they were molded to fit every line of his body, and his fine linen shirt clings to his arms, drawing my eyes to the muscles beneath.

"And for the record, you look much better in your own clothes than you did in my ruffled pajamas."

He grins, his hand over his heart. "Thank the Goddess. I wasn't sure I'd recover from that fashion disaster."

For a moment, we stare at each other awkwardly, yet sweetly. He glances around the room, takes in the bookshelves, the faded tapestry, the drying herbs by the fireplace.

"Cozy," he says.

"Prison-y," I reply.

He gives a low chuckle and then, gradually, his expression becomes more serious. "Roxy... I meant what I said earlier. You're a shifter. You've felt it, haven't you?"

I stiffen. "I've felt... different, maybe. And much better since I stopped taking that awful herb."

He nods. "That's because it's wolfsbane. It's toxic to us. You took too little to kill you but enough to keep you from shifting and to keep your instincts dulled. Your mother's been giving it to you every day, hasn't she?"

"She said it was for my illness." My voice trembles. "To make me better."

He steps closer, his voice gentle. "You're not sick. You're trying to shift. She's been keeping you hidden, Roxy. You've just never been allowed to be who you are."

My breath catches in my chest. I want to argue. I want to tell him he's wrong, that I *can't* be a wolf shifter. But... the truth is, I haven't felt dizzy or achy since I last took the herb, and I feel much stronger with every passing moment.

"Why would she lie to me?" I whisper.

"I don't know." His eyes search mine. "Maybe she was scared. But you don't have to stay here. I want to take you to Moon River, my village. You'll meet others like you. You'll see for yourself."

I blink at him. "You mean... leave? Now?"

He nods. "Now."

I step back, dazed. I've never been out of the tower. The thought of leaving gives me butterflies in my stomach, and something else flutters in my chest, something that draws me to Leo.

"I want to go," I nearly shout.

"Yeah?" His smile is warm.

I nod slowly. "I've *always* wanted to go. Just not without saying goodbye."

He doesn't push. He just waits while I cross to my writing desk, grab a sheet of parchment, and scrawl a short note with a shaking hand.

Mother,

I need to see the world for myself. I promise I'll come back. Please don't worry. I'm safe.

Love,

Roxy

I fold it and place it beside her favorite book on the table. My throat tightens as I look around the tower. My whole life is in this one room. The old velvet chair, my vanity and bed, the kitchen I spend most of my waking hours baking in, and my half-finished embroidery in the basket....

I'm not afraid of the monsters Mother mentioned, not when I know Leo will be with me. I take a deep breath, grab a satchel, and toss in a few pairs of clothes and supplies. When I turn back to Leo, he's pulled a length of rope from the pack on his back.

"Ready?" he asks.

I nod, although I'm not entirely sure if I am. I take his hand anyway.

We secure the rope to the bedpost and lower it out the window, down the stone wall. The wind whips at my hair as I climb over the edge, Leo steadying me from below.

One foot, then the next, step by unsteady step.

I'm climbing out of the tower—for the first time in my life.

We reach the ground. I slip off my boots, feeling the grass, wet and soft under my bare feet as I take my first real steps into the valley beyond the tower.

I'm not walking. I'm running.

Laughing, breathless, I dash down the gentle slope like a child. The breeze wraps around me, lifting my long hair from my shoulders, tugging my skirt against my legs. The scent of wildflowers bursts in the air.

I throw my arms wide and spin in a circle, tilting my head to the sky. Clouds drift high across the moon overhead, and below them, the valley stretches out like a secret world waiting to be discovered.

Leo leans against a tree at the edge of the clearing, watching me with an amused half-smile. He says nothing, just folds his arms and shakes his head like I'm some kind of silly fool.

And maybe I am, but I've *never* felt like this before.

I see the lake up ahead, sparkling midnight blue, cradled between a line of trees and a bed of stones. I glance back at Leo once, and then I'm running again, down to the shore. The water is cold, but I don't care. I hike up my dress and wade up to my knees before splashing forward and falling in with a delighted shriek.

I come up laughing. "It's perfect!"

Leo sits down at the water's edge while I float on my back, my eyes closed, grinning at the sky. This isn't just joy. This is *freedom.*

Eventually, I crawl back onto the stones, soaked and shivering but glowing with satisfaction. I wring out my skirt and hair as best I can.

"All right," he says, glancing at the sky. "We've got to get moving."

I blink. "Already?"

"If we shifted into wolf form, we'd reach Moon River by morning. But you haven't shifted yet, so the route we'd usually take isn't safe. In human form, you wouldn't stand a chance against rogues."

"Rogues?"

He nods. "Enemy wolves. It's safer to stay on the paths and roads now, but that means it'll take us a full day. Maybe a day and a half if the weather turns."

I sigh, glancing back toward the lake, toward the tower beyond the trees. "All right. Let's go."

We put on our cloaks, and I slip my boots back on. Making our way toward a curtain of vines hanging thick over a gap in the cliffs,

Leo walks beside me. As we step through, I feel a sudden pressure in my chest, and the second we cross, the sky blackens.

Lightning flickers in the distance, followed by thunder. Rain starts as a drizzle then a downpour. Cold sheets of it soak us through in minutes, and the path turns muddy and slick. I hold my cloak tight at the neck, squinting into the gray wash as we trudge forward. Leo places his hand gently on my elbow, steadying me, and his presence is comforting.

We walk for hours, and my feet begin to ache. My soaked clothes cling to me, and every so often Leo glances sideways, checking on me without a word.

By the time we reach an inn, I'm so tired I could cry. It's a squat timber building tucked against the side of a mossy hill, firelight flickering behind warped glass windows. The sign reads *The Thistle & Boar*, and smoke curls from the chimney.

Inside, the warmth nearly brings me to my knees. The common room is alive with noisy laughter, clinking mugs, boots thumping against the floorboards. A red headed woman in a green velvet gown is singing in the corner, her voice strong and smooth. A man with an accent and two dogs at his feet tells a story too fast for me to follow. Behind the bar, a stout woman flips a fritter in a skillet with one hand and pours something frothy from a pitcher with the other.

I press closer to Leo, overwhelmed. "Are they all wolf shifters?"

"Some," he murmurs. "Some aren't. But all of them know not to ask too many questions."

Upstairs, our room is small, warm, and dimly lit by a single candle. I peel off my wet cloak and collapse into a chair with a groan.

Leo tosses a log onto the fire then turns his back without a word, so that I can change out of my soaked dress.

I hesitate for only a moment before peeling it off, my teeth chattering, and reaching into my satchel for the slightly damp nightgown I packed. It's not dry, but it's better. I tug it over my head quickly, grateful for Leo's gentle demeanor.

"All done," I say softly.

He glances back, giving me a small nod, then pulls his cloak from his pack and lays it across the wooden floor.

I smile weakly then climb beneath the blanket, curling up on my side as warmth slowly seeps back into my bones. Leo settles on the floor with a quiet sigh, one arm folded beneath his head.

It's quiet for a moment, the fire crackling between us.

"Goodnight, Leo," I whisper.

"Sleep well, Roxy," he says. "We've got a long journey in the morning."

I mean to stay awake, to ask him more about Moon River, to tell him about the lake and how the water made me feel alive for the first time. But my body sinks into the mattress, and sleep swallows me whole.

THE MEADOW IN THE WOODS

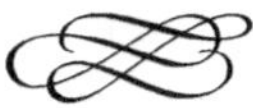

Leo

The scream cuts through my sleep like a blade.

I jolt upright on the floor, my heart pounding, my muscles coiled before I'm even fully awake. For a split second, I don't know where I am, but then I hear her again.

"Roxy!"

She's on the bed, thrashing beneath the blanket, her hands clenched into fists, and her face contorted in pain. Her nightgown is damp with sweat, her hair plastered to her forehead. Her eyes are open but unfocused, wild with terror.

Another scream tears from her throat, high and raw.

I scramble to my feet, but I don't rush her. If I move too fast, I'll scare her even more, and I can't have anyone in this inn thinking I'm the cause of her screaming.

"Roxy," I say gently, keeping my voice low and calm. "You're all right. I'm here."

She doesn't hear me. She's panting, gripping the sheets like they're the only thing keeping her tethered to the earth. She kicks her legs sharply, and for a moment her eyes flash golden, bright and burning.

Her wolf is surfacing.

It's too soon, trying to rip its way out of her while she's half asleep in a borrowed bed.

"Roxy," I repeat, moving slowly toward her. "It's okay. You're not alone."

Her cries soften into choked sobs, but her body's still fighting, still caught in some invisible war. I cross the room slowly, my hands open at my sides.

"You're safe," I murmur. "Breathe, Roxy. Just breathe."

And then something changes. I notice the closer I get, the less she fights. Her eyes move over me, the gold fading back into blue. Her breathing is still ragged, but her fists begin to unclench. She gasps like she's drowning, and I sit gently on the edge of the bed.

"I've got you," I whisper, and she folds into me without hesitation.

She clings to my shirt, trembling violently. Her whole body is slick with sweat and still humming with residual energy, but she's not screaming anymore. Her sobs are quieter now, more human.

"I—I'm sorry," she chokes out, her voice breaking. "I didn't mean to—"

"Shhh." I press my hand to the back of her head, anchoring her to my chest. "It's okay. You didn't do anything wrong."

"I woke you. I—I scared you."

"You didn't scare me." I tuck her tighter into my chest. "You just surprised me. That's all."

I hold her until her breathing evens out, until the trembling slows. Her body curls against mine like she's trying to disappear, and the strange thing is, I don't *really want* to let her go.

I thought I'd never have a mate. I told myself it didn't matter, and that I didn't need anyone. That being Alpha of my pack was enough for me.

But this? This feels like something real.

The way her pain eased as soon as I got close. The way her wolf responded to me even though she's never shifted. The way it feels to hold her, like the Moon Goddess Herself has blessed us.

She sniffles against me. "What's happening to me?"

"You're coming into your wolf," I say gently. "Your first shift is trying to break through. It's probably the wolfsbane leaving your system. It's waking everything up."

"I feel like I'm falling apart," she whispers.

"You're not. You're waking up. It hurts now, but it gets better. I promise."

She's quiet for a moment. Her hand finds mine, and I let our fingers tangle together.

"I'm scared, Leo."

"I know," I say. "But I'm here."

I don't tell her what I'm thinking, that she and I might be destined to be more than just friends. Not yet. Not while she's still fragile, trembling, and barely keeping herself together.

The sun is already climbing by the time we eat breakfast and leave the inn. I carry both of our satchels, and Roxy walks beside me, the color slowly returning to her cheeks. She's quiet, but not withdrawn. She takes in every sight like it might vanish if she looks away. The morning air is fresh and warm, a far cry from the storm that battered us yesterday, and I thank the Goddess for the clear skies. We needed this, especially Roxy.

She lifts her face toward the sun like she's never felt it before, her eyes closed and lips parted slightly in wonder. And I realize she hasn't ever seen the sun, not like this. Not outside, not free.

We don't talk much at first, just the crunch of boots on pebbles and birdsong in the trees. Her long, golden hair shines in the sunlight, damp at the ends from where she tied it back still wet. She's wearing the gown she changed into this morning—pale green, simple, travel-wrinkled—but she makes it look like something royal.

Every few minutes, I glance her way. Still checking, I guess. Making sure she's okay after what happened, and perhaps making sure she's really here.

By late morning, we stop in a meadow ringed with sunflowers and tall grass. A stream cuts through the middle, bubbling over smooth stones. Roxy sits near the edge, pulling off her boots and letting her toes sink into the moss.

I drop the bags and stretch, the sun warming my shoulders.

She glances at me, then down at the grass. "Can I ask you something?"

"Of course."

"Will you show me again?" she says softly. "Your wolf. You were so far away last time...."

My brows lift, surprised—but I nod.

"All right," I say. "But I'll need a second."

She smiles and immediately turns around, facing away. "Not peeking, I swear."

I chuckle and step back into the tree line, tugging off my boots, my shirt, and my belt. In seconds I'm out of my clothes, breathing deep, grounding myself in the scent of the earth, the hum of the air, the shift stirring in my blood.

Then I let go.

Bones crack, sinew twists, heat rushes through me—and in the blink of an eye, I'm no longer standing on two feet.

I shake out my fur, stretch my limbs, and breathe in the world with a wolf's nose. Everything sharpens. Every scent, every rustle of the wind, every beat of her heart in the clearing behind me.

I bark softly.

She turns.

Her eyes grow wide, and for a moment she just stares.

"I forgot how... big you are," she says, and then laughs a little, stepping toward me. "And beautiful."

I huff out a breath and lower my head slightly, my tail swaying as I pad toward her. She reaches out a hand, her fingers brushing my muzzle gently.

"Is it still you in there?" she asks.

I bark once.

She smiles. "Good."

Then, with a sudden laugh, she turns and *runs.*

I don't need more of an invitation.

I chase her, my paws light on the grass, weaving between clumps of wildflowers as she darts, squeals, and laughs. She has no plan—just joy. Her skirt tangles around her legs, and she throws her arms out, spinning in circles before falling backward into the flowers, breathless.

I circle her once, then plop down beside her, my tongue lolling and tail thumping. She lies there staring up at the sky, her chest rising and falling, her hair fanned in the grass.

"I think this is the best day of my life," she murmurs while petting my head and looking into my eyes.

I nuzzle her gently, and she whispers, "I don't know what's happening to me, Leo, but when I'm with you, nothing seems quite as scary."

I rest my head beside hers in the grass, letting the moment stretch. Sunlight dapples the meadow, and for the first time in a long while, everything feels exactly as it should.

Mid-afternoon, I retreat into the trees and shift back, letting the fur slip from my skin and the heat of my wolf settle back into my bones. I dress quickly, tugging on my shirt while trying not to step barefoot on any thorns. Roxy hums to herself as she wanders the edge of the stream, plucking a dandelion and spinning it between her fingers.

She turns when I approach, her smile warm, open. "Thank you for showing me. I'll never forget it."

"You're welcome." I shoulder the packs again and nod toward the path. "Ready to keep going?"

She glances back at the meadow like she's saying goodbye to a dream, then falls into step beside me. "Ready."

We walk for hours, the world slowly turning from warm gold to soft blue. The trees grow denser, the path narrower, and I know we're close. Roxy doesn't complain, even though her feet must be aching. She listens intently when I point out signs of deer or the faint claw marks on a tree from a patrolling wolf. Her eyes are wide, curious, soaking in every detail like she's afraid it'll vanish.

When the sun finally dips below the horizon, and shadows stretch long across the trail, I stop and glance toward the ridge ahead. "We're close," I say. "Just a few more miles that way, and we'll cross into Moon River territory."

Her eyes brighten with a mix of excitement and nerves.

"But we can't travel at night," I add, setting down the bags. "Too risky. Rogues, unstable terrain, wandering beasts. We'll make camp here and finish the trip in the morning."

She nods and starts gathering kindling while I clear a small patch of ground. Once the fire is crackling and the light dances over her face, I pull out dried meat from my pack and hand her a strip. She takes it delicately, sniffing it before chewing, and I suppress a grin.

"It's not bad," she says around a bite. "Chewy."

I chuckle and settle beside her on the blanket, the fire warming our knees. "Glad it meets your expectations."

The stars start to appear, one by one, and the hush of night falls over the woods. Frogs croak, cicadas sing, and in the distance, an owl hoots. Roxy leans back on her elbows, her hair tumbling over her shoulders, ending in a pool by her hips.

"I've never seen so many stars," she murmurs, looking up. "They're everywhere."

"You don't get skies like this from a tower window."

"No," she says softly. "You really don't."

We sit like that for a while, not speaking, just listening to the fire and the forest breathe around us. She curls her legs beneath her and rests her head against my shoulder without asking, and I let her. My arm naturally wraps around her, holding her close.

Roxy turns. "Do you really think I'll shift?"

"I do," I say. "It's in you. You're close—I can feel it."

She's quiet for a long moment. Then, "It hurts."

"I know." I brush a lock of hair behind her ear. "But it only hurts for a moment. I'll be with you when it happens. I won't let you go through it alone."

Her hand finds mine in the dark. "Thank you."

My heart gives a small, traitorous thud.

I didn't expect this—her. This strange, stubborn, brave girl with stars in her eyes and decades of loneliness pressing against her heart.

Now that I've found her, I'm not sure I'll ever be able to walk away.

The fire flickers low, and the stars keep watch. Beside me, Roxy leans into my side, completely unaware that I might already be falling for her.

THE BABY IN THE LEGEND

THE FIRE CASTS SOFT AMBER LIGHT ON LEO'S FACE. WE SIT SHOULDER to shoulder in the clearing, the stars like scattered silver dust overhead. Everything smells like trees, smoke, and earth, and it feels peaceful.

I hug my knees to my chest and tip my head back to stare at the sky. "Today really was the best day of my life."

Leo glances at me, his brow lifted slightly, amused. "Is that so? It started off a little rough."

I laugh. "Other than how I woke you up, of course. I ran barefoot through a meadow with a beautiful wolf, ate trail jerky in the moonlight, and got to see the whole, big sky." I smile softly. "For someone who's spent her entire life behind stone walls, that's… magical."

He chuckles, low and warm. "Well, I'm honored to have spent it with you. And I suppose… it wasn't too terrible for me either."

I nudge him with my elbow, and he grins. But the laughter fades from my lips as a heavier thought returns—the one that's been sitting in the back of my mind all day.

"Leo?" I stare into the flames. "Why would my mother give me something that made me sick?"

His smile fades.

"I've been taking that herb, *wolfsbane*, you called it, since I was little. Anytime I felt strange, sick or... restless, she made me eat that bitter herb, telling me it would help, and that it was medicine."

Leo doesn't answer right away. I can feel his body tense beside mine.

"I didn't question her," I go on. "Not ever. I thought she was protecting me. But now... now that I've stopped taking it, I feel so much better. Stronger. Like something inside me is—waking up."

"It is," Leo says softly. "It's your wolf."

I look over at him, searching his face. "What would happen if *you* took it?"

He hesitates for only a second. "If I took enough?" He meets my eyes. "I'd die."

The words hit me like a slap. I blink, unsure if I heard him right. "Die?"

He nods. "Wolfsbane is poison to us. It burns through our blood, shuts down everything that makes us who we are. You were getting tiny doses, just enough to keep your instincts buried. But it could have killed you."

I turn away from him, blinking back tears. "Why?" I whisper. "Why would she give me that?"

Leo doesn't answer.

The silence stretches, thick and awful. I can feel his hesitation. Whatever he's holding back, he doesn't want to say it. But I need to know.

"Leo," I say again, this time more firmly. "Tell me."

He sighs. "I don't think she's your real mother, Roxy."

The whole world tilts. My breath catches in my throat. "What?"

"I didn't want to say anything until I was sure, but everything you've told me—the tower, the isolation, the wolfsbane... it all adds up."

I shake my head slowly, trying to process. "Of course, she's my mother. She loves me. I love her. She raised me. She sang to me. She braided my hair every morning. She's *my mother.*"

"Roxy," Leo says gently. "Someone who loves you wouldn't poison you or keep you hidden. They wouldn't lie to you about who you are or keep you locked up."

I press a hand to my mouth, my heart thudding wildly. The firelight flickers across my skin, but I feel cold all over. "I don't understand," I whisper.

"You're a shifter," he says. "That's in your blood, your bones. It's not something she could've missed. Not for twenty-one years. She had to know. And she kept you away from your people, Roxy. From your pack. From your true self."

"If she's not my real mother... then who am I?"

Leo moves a little closer, his hand resting lightly over mine. I don't pull away.

The stars still shine above us, but nothing feels the same. Everything has changed. I sit frozen, Leo's hand over mine, but my thoughts are miles away—chasing shadows and unraveling the seams of everything I've ever known.

"Roxy," he says gently. "There's something else I need to tell you."

I glance at him, but I don't speak. I can't. My throat is too tight.

He watches me for a moment and then begins.

"There's a legend," he says. "Something our elders still whisper of when they think no one's listening, but we weren't allowed to speak of as pups. It happened nearly twenty-one years ago."

My pulse jumps at the number.

He goes on, his voice low, steady. "An Alpha and his Luna had just had their first child, a baby girl with long golden enchanted hair with strands of red like yours, a trait of their pack."

I swallow hard, staring at him, not daring to interrupt.

"But the child's power wasn't a secret. A coven of witches came to the Alpha with a warning: hand over the girl, or they'd wipe out the entire pack."

My stomach turns. "That's... horrible."

Leo nods grimly. "It was. The Alpha fought them, of course. Refused at first. But the witches made good on their threat. They killed them all."

I press a hand to my chest, feeling my heart pound like it's trying to escape.

"In the end," Leo continues, "the Alpha gave in. He and the Luna handed over their child and the witches returned life to the pack."

My voice is barely a whisper. "What happened to the baby?"

"No one knows," he says. "She vanished. The witches disappeared with her. The pack mourned her like she was dead."

I stare up at the sky, my mind spinning.

Long golden hair. Twenty-one years ago. A stolen baby.

"But that's just a story," I say quickly, trying to outrun the wild thoughts racing through my mind. "Right? A legend?"

Leo looks at me, something unreadable in his eyes. "Stories come from somewhere, Roxy. They might get twisted over time, but the bones are often true."

I shake my head weakly, unsure. "That can't be me. That baby can't be me."

"Why not?" he asks gently.

"Because—" I pause. "Because I was raised in the tower. By *Mother*. She said my father died in a war. That I was born sickly. That's why I couldn't leave."

"And yet she kept you hidden. Gave you wolfsbane. Lied to you."

I think of my hair. The way *Mother* always braids it when she's feeling under the weather and then perks right back up.

"Roxy," Leo says, watching me closely. "Have you ever healed quickly?"

I nod, slowly. I think of how my bruises and scrapes fade within hours. "Always. I thought... I thought it was normal."

"It's not. Not for humans. And the witches—if the story's true—they wanted you for what your hair can do. There's magic in it. Healing. Longevity. Maybe more."

I pull my hair over one shoulder, staring at it like it's something foreign.

Could it really be true? Could I be that baby? Could I be... a wolf shifter?

"You don't have to believe it all right now. But the truth has been hidden from you for a long time."

I nod slowly, the weight of it all sinking in.

Leo stiffens beside me. One second, we're still sitting at the fire, and the next, he's on his feet, his eyes scanning the darkness beyond the trees.

"What is it?" I ask, my voice barely above a whisper.

He doesn't answer right away. His nostrils flare and his body goes tense. Then, very softly, he mutters, "Rogues."

My breath catches. "What?"

"Two of them. Close." His gaze jerks to the woods behind me. "Get up."

I scramble to my feet, my heart pounding, and before I can even ask where to run, he grabs my hand and pulls me toward the nearest tree with low-hanging branches.

"Climb. Now."

"What—?"

"No time," he growls. "Roxy, *climb*."

I obey, grabbing the lowest limb and hauling myself up, the rough bark scraping my palms. He boosts me higher until I can swing my legs up and wedge myself against the trunk. The tree sways with my movements, but it holds. From here, I can see Leo standing in the clearing.

His transformation is swift, violent and graceful all at once. Bones snap, muscles twist, and in a blink, the man I was just speaking to is gone, replaced by the massive black wolf.

Two wolves slink out of the trees, gray-brown, lean, their ribs visible under their ragged fur. Their eyes gleam with malice.

They circle Leo, sniffing, snarling low in their throats. They're not just hunting. They're *looking* for someone.

Leo growls once, low, deep, and threatening. The rogues don't flinch. One lunges. Leo meets it mid-air.

The sound of impact echoes through the meadow. Fur, claws, teeth, tumble in a blur, snarling and snapping. The other rogue charges in, trying to flank him, but Leo twists, throwing the first wolf off with a powerful shove of his shoulders and meeting the second head-on.

My heart is in my throat. He's fighting both of them alone. I can't look away from my perch in the tree. I cling to a branch with shaking hands, in awe of him as I watch him fight.

Leo moves like he was born for battle. Every motion is practiced, deadly. He's bigger than both rogues, but they're fast, relentless, wild with rage.

The first wolf snaps at his hind leg. Leo spins and sinks his teeth into the rogue's shoulder, tearing flesh. The wolf howls and retreats, but the second slams into Leo's side, its jaws clamping onto his shoulder.

I cry out, even though I think he won't hear me.

Leo doesn't fall. He throws his weight sideways, slamming the rogue into the dirt, and then, with a vicious snarl, he bites down— hard.

The rogue yelps once and then goes limp.

Leo doesn't pause. He whirls on the first wolf, blood slick on his muzzle.

The last rogue hesitates, its ears back, but it's too late. Leo pounces. It's over in seconds. Both wolves lie still, the clearing quiet. I sit frozen in the tree, my breath caught in my throat.

He just saved my life.

Leo lifts his head, his muzzle glinting red in the moonlight. His eyes meet mine through the shadows. He's still a wolf. Still fierce, bloodied, bristling with the aftermath of battle.

But I'm not afraid.

I lower myself slowly from the tree, dropping to the ground with shaking knees. He pads toward me, his massive paws silent on the forest floor, stopping just short of touching me.

I reach out with trembling fingers.

He leans forward, pressing his forehead to my palm.

"Thank you," I whisper, voice cracking. "Thank you for saving me."

His wolf form exhales a low rumble—something deep and soft, almost… comforting.

And somehow, in my mind I hear him say, *"I always will."*

THE MAGIC IN THE HAIR

Leo

I LIMP BACK TOWARD THE CAMPFIRE, ONE PAW DRAGGING SLIGHTLY WITH each step. Blood drips from my shoulder, hot and sticky against my fur. The clearing smells like blood—mine and theirs.

Behind me, Roxy's footsteps crunch softly through the underbrush. I stop near our satchels and glance over my shoulder. She's watching me, her lips parted, worry painted across her face.

"*Roxy,*" I say through the mind-link, pushing the words gently in her direction. "*Turn around so I can shift.*"

I don't know if it'll work. She's not from my pack. But still, without hesitation, she turns.

She heard me, but it shouldn't be possible. The connection shouldn't be there, unless….

I don't let myself follow the thought. Not now.

I shift.

Bones snap. The pain in my shoulder intensifies for one white-hot second, and then I'm kneeling in the grass, naked, blood running freely down my arm. My body hums with exhaustion and adrenaline. My hands shake as I reach for my clothes.

Behind me, Roxy doesn't move. Doesn't peek.

My fingers fumble with my pants, but I manage. I tug on my shirt last, wincing as the fabric brushes over the wound on my upper arm. The bite is deep, raw and angry, still seeping blood. I need to clean it soon, but it's not life-threatening.

"I'm dressed," I say, my voice hoarse.

She turns slowly. Her eyes go straight to the wound, and she gasps softly. "Leo—"

"I'm all right." I sit down beside the fire, easing myself down with a hiss through my teeth. "Just a bite."

She kneels next to me without asking, her fingers already moving toward the bloodied fabric at my shoulder. "It's still bleeding."

"I've had worse."

"Doesn't mean you should ignore it."

I don't stop her as she rips open the cloth, inspecting the bite. Her touch is gentle, but her hands are shaking.

I glance at her face, her eyes wide. Her skin is pale, and her lips are pressed together like she's holding back everything she wants to say.

"You did hear me," I say quietly. "In your mind."

She nods. "Yes. I don't know how, but I did."

I exhale. That confirms it. No one outside my pack should be able to receive a link from me unless we're connected, and there's only one kind of bond strong enough to cross those lines.

The mate bond.

"I'll heal it," she says, already reaching for her hair. "Just sit still."

"You don't have to—"

"I want to."

I fall silent and let her take care of me. As she braids strands of hair around my arm, she whispers, "You fought for me."

"I'd do it again," I say.

She meets my eyes for a heartbeat, and in hers, I see something new. Trust.

Her hair heals my wound, and for a moment, as her fingers brush my skin, I don't feel like an Alpha carrying a stranger to safety. I feel like a man sitting beside the one the Moon Goddess chose for him.

When she's finished, she sits back on her heels. "There," she says softly.

"Thank you."

She nods but doesn't move away, and I don't either.

"You're not alone anymore, Roxy."

Her eyes glisten. "Neither are you."

I tamp down the sudden urge to kiss her. It's too soon, too much. I won't risk pushing her away.

Glancing toward the trees where the rogues came from, every muscle in my body tightens, even though I'm bone-deep tired. The fight's over, but my instincts are screaming that it's not safe to stay here.

I glance at Roxy. She's sitting close with her arms wrapped around her knees, watching the shadows like they might move again. Her braid has come loose, and tendrils curl around her cheeks. She looks shaken.

"We can't stay here," I say quietly. "There are more out there. Maybe not close yet, but they'll smell the blood. We can't risk another ambush."

I push myself slowly to my feet. "We need to move. Get to Moon River before dawn."

We stamp out the remains of the fire, grinding the embers to ash. As we start moving through the forest, moonlight breaks through in patches.

I glance sideways at Roxy. "You doing okay?"

She nods. Her breath puffs white in the cool air. "I'm tired, but I'll make it."

The forest thins as we climb, but the path is rough, with gnarled roots, loose rocks, and uneven ground. Still, Roxy keeps pace, her steps sure, focused.

"I'll feel better once we're past that hill," I say, pointing ahead. "That's where Moon River territory starts."

"Is it guarded?"

"Always. Patrols switch every few hours. They'll scent us before we arrive. If they catch my trail, they'll meet us."

"And if they don't?"

"I'll call them."

She nods again, not missing a beat.

As we climb the next rise, I glance at the sky. The stars have started to fade. A faint rim of light is gathering on the horizon, just a hint of the dawn to come. We're moving fast enough. We'll make it home soon, but I still don't let my guard down.

The trail winds downward again, and through the trees ahead I glimpse the glint of the river, silver and winding like a ribbon. Just beyond that lies home.

"Almost there," I whisper.

We've barely rounded the bend when I hear them.

"Alpha?" Kiana's voice, clear and focused, comes through the mind-link. *"We caught your scent. Are you safe?"*

"I'm safe." I send back. *"I've got someone with me. We're on the north ridge trail, headed toward the village. Can you meet us?"*

Corwin answers next. His tone is calm, as always. *"Less than a mile out. Kiana, Harla, and I are coming."*

Beside me, Roxy glances over. "Are you all right?"

"I'm great. We will be even better in a minute," I say. "Three members of my pack picked up my scent and mind-linked with me."

Roxy looks surprised. "Where are they?"

"They're close by. They'll take us home."

She pulls the satchel higher on her shoulder, her jaw tightening. "Will they be okay with me?"

I stop, turning toward her. "Of course, they will."

She nods, but I can see the worry behind her eyes.

A moment later, Kiana breaks through the brush, sleek, silver-gray, her eyes sharp and alert. Corwin lopes in behind her, with silver with streaks of black in his tail. He's broad-shouldered, his stride steady. Harla is last, the color of fresh snowfall. They surround us in seconds, not threatening but protective. All three warriors turn as one, their ears up. Corwin sends the signal, and the three of them take positions. Kiana in front, Harla trailing, Corwin at my right, the three of them in a loose triangle.

I glance at Roxy. "We're walking with protection now. Just stay close."

She nods quickly and steps beside me, her eyes darting between the wolves like she's still not sure if this is real.

We start down the trail, the guards around us moving silent and steady. Every now and then, Kiana veers off, checking the brush. Harla scans the trees, her steps silent as shadow. Corwin matches my pace stride for stride, his head low, listening.

The sky is softening–first gray then pink. The smell of home grows thick in my nose, woodsmoke, and bread baking in the distance.

Roxy catches her breath when we reach the final ridge.

Moon River spreads out before us, tucked into a crescent of land beneath the mountain. Chimneys puff into the sky. Early risers move through the main street, hauling buckets, opening shutters. It's still sleepy, safe.

My chest tightens. "That's home."

Roxy is still staring. Her eyes are full of wonder, when I murmur, "Welcome to Moon River."

And for the first time in days, the weight on my shoulders feels lighter.

THE FRIENDS IN THE VILLAGE

Roxy

THE TREES THIN JUST AS THE SKY BEGINS TO BLUSH WITH MORNING light. I blink against the golden haze spilling through the forest, and then suddenly, it's there.

Moon River Village.

Nestled between two hills, it's the most peaceful, beautiful place I've ever seen. Neat rows of cottages with moss-covered roofs and flower boxes line the winding paths. Smoke puffs lazily from the stone chimneys, and a gentle stream winds through the heart of it all, sparkling in the dawn.

Everything about it feels right, like I've been waiting for this place my whole life.

I slow without realizing it, taking in the scene. It's nothing like the cold stone tower I came from. The village feels warm and alive. Quilts hang from open windows, chickens peck along a garden path, and somewhere nearby, someone is singing.

The three wolves who escorted us, sleek and graceful, each of them beautiful in their own wild way, pad a few steps ahead of me and Leo. Their fur glows gold in the morning sun as they come to a stop at the edge of the main path. One by one, they lower their heads and bow deeply to Leo.

He doesn't say a word, just gives them a small nod in return. It's clear they understand. Without another sound, the three wolves turn and run off down the hill, disappearing into the trees. I watch them go, something like awe and reverence tightening in my chest.

A man and woman appear from one of the roads up ahead. The man is tall and strong, bearded, with silver at his temples and calm brown eyes. The woman beside him is beautiful, with coppery curls and a big smile that reaches her green eyes. She's holding a wrapped bundle of something warm, the scent of cinnamon drifting toward us.

Leo smiles. "Marek. Hanna."

The man grins. "You look like hell, Leo."

"Rough night," Leo mutters, then he gestures toward me. "This is Roxy."

Marek's expression shifts instantly, softening, respectful. "It's an honor to meet you, Roxy."

Hanna steps forward with a smile and gently presses the bundle into my hands. "You must be starving. Fresh cinnamon bread."

My fingers close around the warm cloth. "Thank you. You're so kind."

"You're safe now," Hanna says, placing a hand on my shoulder. "Come inside. We've made a place for you."

I glance at Leo, and he nods. I step inside their home, clutching the bread close to my chest like it might anchor me to their world. For the first time in my life, I'm not behind a locked door. I'm not hidden. I'm not being poisoned, or silenced, or shrinking into shadows. I'm walking into the heart of a village under the open sky, and some-how... it feels like coming home, and these people feel like family.

Warmth and the smell of cinnamon wrap around me as I go further into Marek and Hanna's home. The cottage is cozy, with a fire in the hearth and beams of early sunlight filtering through white linen curtains. The walls are lined with shelves full of books, dried herbs, and handmade trinkets. Everything feels lived-in and loved.

Hanna gestures for me to sit at the wooden table while she sets down plates of bacon and eggs and then slices the warm cinnamon bread. Marek pours coffee into mismatched mugs and offers one to Leo, who accepts it gratefully and sinks into the chair beside me.

I sit across from Hanna, sipping the deliciously warm coffee.

"Eat," she says with a smile. "You've earned it."

I glance at Leo, who's already tearing into the bread with one hand and nursing his coffee with the other. He nods encouragingly.

I take a bite and instantly melt. "This is… unbelievable."

"It's a family recipe," Hanna says with a wink.

We eat in companionable silence for a few minutes, the tension of the journey slowly easing in the comfort of food and friendship, but I can feel the questions waiting heavy in the air.

Leo finally breaks the silence. "We ran into rogues last night. Two of them."

Marek frowns. "Close to the border?"

Leo nods. "They caught our scent while we were camped. We didn't have time to wait for sunrise. We headed straight here."

"You okay?" Hanna asks gently, looking at me.

I swallow then nod. "I think so. I've never seen anything like that before. Leo protected me."

"She was brave," Leo says. "Stayed in a tree until it was safe. And… she healed my wound afterward."

That gets Marek's attention. He leans forward, his eyes narrowing slightly. "Healed you?"

I move a little under their gaze. "My hair. It heals…."

"It's part of what makes her special," Leo says quietly.

I lower my eyes, unsure how to respond.

"She was raised in a tower," Leo continues. "Kept isolated. Lied to. Her mother—who may not actually be her mother—fed her wolfsbane."

Hanna gasps. "Wolfsbane?"

"She thought it was medicine," Leo says. "Tiny doses, since childhood."

Marek's jaw tightens. "That explains a lot."

"I've never shifted," I add softly. "I didn't even know I was a shifter until a few days ago. I thought the restlessness, the aches, the... dreams were just sickness."

"You were drugged to keep your wolf from surfacing," Hanna says gently, reaching across the table to squeeze my hand. "That's not your fault."

"I know that now," I whisper. "But it's still hard to believe."

Leo sets down his mug and turns to Marek. "Has there been any word of Silas?"

He shakes his head, the tension returning to his features. "Nothing yet. It's been almost a week."

"He was supposed to return nights ago," Leo mutters, mostly to himself.

"Could he have been killed?" Hanna asks.

"He's smart," Marek says. "Cautious. But if rogues are pushing this close to the village..."

"We'll find him," Leo says firmly, but I can hear the worry in his voice.

A heavy silence settles over the table.

Hanna stands and clears the dishes then gives me a soft smile. "Come, Roxy. You need sleep."

I glance at Leo. He gives me a tired smile. "Go. Rest."

"You, too," Hanna scolds Leo gently. "You're no good to anyone with your eyes half shut."

He huffs out a quiet laugh. "Yes, ma'am."

Hanna leads me down a short hallway to a small room with a bed tucked beneath a window and a quilt folded neatly at the foot. It smells like roses, and a small table holds a bowl of fresh water and a stack of folded clothes.

She smooths the blankets. "It's not much, but it's yours as long as you need it."

"It's perfect," I whisper, my throat tight.

She touches my shoulder. "Sleep now. We'll talk more later."

I nod, and she leaves me in the quiet.

Leo's voice drifts softly from the doorway. "I'll see you tonight."

I turn to find him leaning on the doorframe, a gentleness in his eyes that makes my chest ache.

"Thank you, Leo. For everything."

He nods. "Rest now. I'll be close."

And then he's gone.

I sink into the bed, pull the quilt over my shoulders, and close my eyes.

I WAKE TO THE SOFT CREAK OF A DOOR AND THE SCENT OF ROSES STILL clinging to the quilt. For a moment, I don't remember where I am. Then I hear Hanna's voice, and the memories of Moon River flood back in.

She pokes her head into the room with a bright smile. "Good, you're awake. I didn't want to rush you, but I've got exciting news."

I sit up slowly, brushing the sleep from my eyes. "What is it?"

She practically glows. "Leo sent word. He wants you to join him for dinner tonight."

Dinner… with Leo? Why would that be exciting? We've had something like dinner before…

Hanna steps inside holding a soft pink dress over her arm, trimmed with delicate white lace and a little white sash at the waist. "You didn't think we were letting you go in travel-wrinkled clothes, did you?"

I laugh nervously. "Is this a date?"

She lifts her brows with delight. "With the Alpha King? Oh, I certainly hope so. Come on. Get up. Let's make you sparkle."

"The Alpha… you mean Leo is the leader of your pack?"

She laughs softly, as if she thought I already knew. "Of course. He's the leader of Moon River."

I stare at her. "But… he's so—humble. He doesn't act like a king."

Hanna nods, her smile fond. "That's what makes him a good leader. He's kind. Protective. Humble. Never puts himself above others, even though he's stronger than most. Leo doesn't have to raise his voice to be respected."

I look down at my hands, my heart beating a little faster. The idea of Leo as the Alpha—powerful, respected, a protector of an entire pack—it makes something flutter deep in my chest.

"He acts as though he's the same as everyone. The king carried my satchel? And slept on the floor?" I whisper.

"Exactly," Hanna says. "And that's why everyone here trusts him. He's selfless, and he leads with his heart."

I bite my lip, warmth blooming across my cheeks. The more I learn about Leo, the more I feel myself sinking, falling, into something like admiration, and so much more.

Hanna hums as she helps me wash my face and brush out my hair. Her hands are gentle and skilled as she styles my hair into a stunning fishbone braid. She laces the dress up my back and dabs something floral behind my ears.

"You know," she says as she adjusts the sash, "Leo's never invited anyone to his home like this. Not for dinner. Not alone."

My heart thuds. "Really?"

Hanna beams. "You're special, Roxy. He sees it. So do I. You've been through so much."

I don't know what to say to that, so I smile and whisper, "Thank you."

Marek and Hanna escort me to Leo's home, which is set on top of a slight hill. It's a stone and timber structure that looks both grand and welcoming. Lanterns glow on the porch, casting a soft golden light across the pathway lined with flowering shrubs. The front door opens as I approach, and a tall, smiling woman in an apron greets me.

"Miss Roxy? The Alpha King is expecting you."

I bid my new friends farewell and step inside. I nearly gasp. The interior is breathtaking, with dark wood floors, handwoven rugs, walls lined with bookshelves and paintings. A fire is lit in the sitting room, and the scent of roasted meat and fresh herbs drifts from the kitchen. It's elegant, warm, beautiful, and comforting.

Leo appears at the top of the stairs wearing a dark gray shirt, black slacks, and a wide smile. "You look..." He stops, takes another step down, and lets out a breath. "Gorgeous."

I feel my cheeks heat as he offers his arm. "Thank you," I say softly.

He leads me to a dining room where a table for two is set with candles, fresh black and white calla lilies, and polished silver. A servant quietly brings in plates of roasted venison, wild vegetables, and fresh bread still steaming.

"I don't think I've ever eaten like this," I admit as I breathe it all in.

"I wanted it to be special," Leo says, watching me carefully. "You deserve something special."

The food is amazing, but it's not what I appreciate most. It's Leo— his voice, the way he listens when I talk, how his eyes crinkle when I make him laugh. He asks reel questions about my childhood, my thoughts on the village, what I dream about now that my world has opened up.

Being near him feels like sitting in the sun after years in the dark.

"I didn't know people could be like this," I say quietly over dessert, some kind of sweet berry tart that melts on my tongue.

"Like what?" he asks.

"Kind. Honest. Safe."

Leo's gaze softens. "You've been through more than anyone should, but you're here now, and you're not alone."

I can't speak for a moment, afraid my voice will crack. I just nod, smile, and reach for his hand across the table. His fingers curl around mine without hesitation.

I'm not sure what this is, just dinner, or something more, but I've never felt safer, or more seen, than I do when I'm with him.

THE FESTIVAL ON THE BIRTHDAY

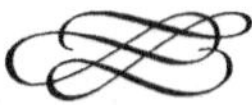

Roxy

THE STARS ARE SCATTERED LIKE GLITTER ACROSS THE SKY, AND THE night is crisp; I tug my cloak closer around me. Leo walks beside me, just close enough that our arms brush now and then.

Dinner was lovely and full of laughter. I didn't expect to feel so comfortable with him, or anyone, this soon. I don't want the evening to end.

When we reach Hanna and Marek's porch, I wonder why Leo doesn't ask me to stay with him, and as though reading my thoughts, he breaks the silence.

"You could, uh... stay with me, but—my pack, they'd probably make a bigger deal out of it than it is," he says, scratching the back of his head, clearly flustered. "I just mean—they'd gossip. About a woman sleeping over. At my place. Which has... never actually happened before."

He looks so awkward I can't help but smile. It's honestly kind of adorable.

Just then, the door clicks open. Marek must've heard us coming.

He opens it, nodding at both of us. "Evening," he says. Then he adds, "Come in for coffee?"

I glance at Leo. He doesn't speak for me, just waits. I like that about him. I nod. "Sure. That sounds nice."

Inside, the house is warm and cozy. It smells like nutmeg and cinnamon. Hanna's already pouring coffee into mugs and smiling like she knows something I don't.

We settle in the living room. Hanna and I sit on the couch while Leo and Marek take the chairs across from us.

Leo sets his mug down after a few quiet sips and says, "I've been thinking. We should head out in the morning. Take a scouting party east—up toward the ridge and the river bend. I want to be sure everything's clear before the festival."

Marek leans forward slightly. "How far out?"

"Far enough we might not be back till late. Maybe not until the next morning."

I try not to frown, but something tightens in my chest. I don't want him to go. Not because I think I'll fall apart without him—I've been alone plenty. But because the idea of him out there, exposed and away, doesn't sit right.

Leo glances at Hanna next. "While we're gone, I need you to make sure Roxy is protected at all times."

Hanna nods. "Of course. She'll be fine with me."

For the first time, it really hits me—I'm actually in *real* danger. If my mother isn't truly my mother–and she's a witch from some hidden coven—then they're probably looking for me. Tracking me. And if they find me here, what happens to Moon River? What happens to Leo, to Hanna, to everyone who's opened their arms to me without knowing the risk? No wonder Leo's suddenly so serious. He's not just being overprotective. He's trying to shield his people from whatever darkness might be following me like a shadow I never even knew I had.

Suddenly, my stomach knots with guilt. I realize they're still talking, but I've completely lost track of the conversation.

Leo looks at Hanna again. "The full moon festival's in two days. Keep the plans moving forward."

"We will," Hanna says, looking at me. "Roxy, would you like to help us plan the festival?"

"Yes, that sounds great." I force a smile, but inside, I feel like a burden.

"We'll make it beautiful," Hanna promises.

Leo stands, slow and steady, and sets his mug down. "We leave at dawn."

I stand, too, walking him to the door.

Outside, the air is cooler, with the kind of quiet that settles deep into your bones. I look up at him. "Be safe, Leo," I say, my hand lightly resting on his chest.

He covers it with his own. His hand is warm. "Always."

I want to ask him to stay, or I want to ask to go with him, but instead, I watch him walk away, into the darkness, the sound of his footsteps swallowed by the woods. And I already miss him.

I SLEEP BETTER THAN I EXPECT TO.

Maybe it's the warmth of the blankets Hanna piled on my bed or the faint scent of roses lingering on the pillow. Maybe it's pure exhaustion.

I dream of Leo. Not in perfect detail, just flashes. His hand in mine. The sound of his laugh. The way his eyes darken when he looks at me like I'm something worth protecting.

When I wake, the sky outside is barely touched by light. I stretch under the covers, listening to the muffled voices downstairs, the clink of mugs, and the low rumble of boots on wood. They're getting ready to leave.

I pull on a sweater and make my way to the kitchen. Leo is already here.

"Good morning," I murmur, still groggy.

He turns when he hears me. "Didn't mean to wake you."

"You didn't," I say, and it's mostly true. "I wanted to say goodbye."

Marek grabs another pack from the floor. "We'll be back tomorrow evening, hopefully before dark."

Leo steps close to me, and I tilt my head to meet his gaze. His hand finds my elbow. It's such a small touch, but it roots me to the floor. "Take care of yourself," he says softly.

"You too." For a second, I think he's going to kiss me. His eyes drop to my mouth, then flicker back up—and he pulls away. Instead, he hugs me and turns to leave.

Marek kisses Hanna goodbye, and with that, he and Leo are gone.

The silence stretches for a breath before Hanna exhales and claps her hands together. "All right. You want to help me plan a party?"

I blink at her. "The Full Moon Festival?"

"Yes, it's one of the most important nights of the year," she says, rolling up her sleeves and pulling out a worn leather-bound notebook. "Festival planning. We've got a lot to do and not enough time to do it."

I smile and wrap my hands around my coffee mug.

"Let's talk food first." Hanna flips through the pages. "That's what everyone's really excited about anyway."

I grin. "Now you're speaking my language."

Hanna turns to a page filled with scribbled notes and little flour smudges in the corners. "Okay, so we've got three big pots of stew planned—one venison, one rabbit, and one with ham and beans. Corwin's wife, Aisha, and her two daughters are handling the bread and sweet rolls. My sister Sasha is bringing honey cakes, and I volunteered us to do the berry cobbler."

I blink. "Us?"

She arches an eyebrow. "Unless you plan to vanish between now and tomorrow night."

I laugh. "Fine. Cobbler duty accepted."

"Good." She scribbles something with a pencil. "Now, drinks. There'll be cider, warm and cold, a few crates of wine, and someone promised to make elderberry lemonade for the kids."

"And what about something stronger?" I ask mischievously.

Hanna gives me a surprised look. "Marek's got a barrel of something stashed that I'm not supposed to talk about. He'll bring it out once the moon is high and the music gets wild."

I shake my head, grinning. "Sounds dangerous."

"Exactly. Have you tasted anything strong before?" she asks.

Without really thinking, I say, "No, but the night of the full moon is also my twenty-first birthday, and I've always wanted to try a sip of something strong to celebrate."

Hanna's head snaps up. "Wait—what?"

I laugh softly at her expression. "Tomorrow. The night of the festival, it's also my birthday."

"Roxy," she says, eyes twinkling. "You didn't say anything."

"I wasn't going to," I admit. "I've never had a real party before."

She stares at me then narrows her eyes. "Well, *that* won't do."

I hold up my hands. "No surprises. Please."

"No promises," she says with a wicked grin, flipping to a clean page. "I just need to jot a few *completely unrelated* notes that have nothing to do with birthday celebrations."

I groan, but I'm smiling, too. "You're relentless."

"Someone has to be," she says, laughing. "Okay, next is the music. The usual group is playing, and I'm sure more will join. I think I'll have them set up in the gazebo so everyone can hear them from all corners of the villages."

"Perfect." I nod.

I glance toward the window where the afternoon light is starting to slant gold across the trees. "This feels like the first time in a while that I'm... looking forward to something."

Hanna's pencil pauses, and she glances at me. "It's nice, isn't it? Knowing something good is coming."

I nod slowly. "It's more than nice."

For the next hour, we keep going, fine-tuning who's responsible for what and making a list of anything still missing. There's a comforting rhythm to it—the quiet scratching of Hanna's pencil, the occasional sip of coffee, the way she thinks out loud and lets me interrupt whenever something pops into my head.

At one point, she starts telling me about a past festival where Marek's brother got so drunk he brought a goat dressed in orange polka dotted ribbons and declared it the moon's chosen companion. I'm laughing so hard I nearly spit out my drink.

"This one'll be better," she says when we finally settle back. "The food, the music, the warmth—it'll all be for the people who made it through. And now, also for you."

Something flickers in my chest at that. Not fear, not worry—just a quiet kind of joy. Like maybe I've finally found my place. "I can't wait," I say, and I mean it.

I don't know what tomorrow will look like, but for the first time in a long time, I'm actually looking forward to finding out. I just hope my being here doesn't put any of these wonderful people at risk.

I'm on the porch with Hanna, putting the finishing touches on a banner we made, when Marek and Leo appear at the edge of the trees. The sun's low, the sky painted in purples and golds, but I can still see it clearly—Leo's entire posture is different. Rigid. Coiled. On edge.

"Something's wrong," Hanna murmurs beside me, already setting down the spool of fabric.

They reach us a moment later. Marek gives Hanna a quick nod and mutters something about needing to check patrol routes. But Leo? He barely looks at anyone except for me.

"Can I talk to you?" he says. His voice is low, tight.

My stomach sinks. "Of course."

We step away from Marek and Hanna's porch.

"What happened?" I ask.

Leo doesn't answer right away. He just runs a hand through his hair and paces across the yard like a caged animal.

"Leo."

"There was something out there," he says finally, his voice low and tense. "Too many broken tracks, strange scents. Then—out of nowhere—rogues. We fought most of them off, but they were on us before we even knew they were close. That doesn't happen, Roxy.

We're trained to catch the signs—smell them coming. But this time... something was different. Something was assisting them...."

"What kind of something?"

He shakes his head. "I don't know yet. That's the problem. But they took Corwin and Harla this time. They just vanished in the fog."

I wait for more, but he doesn't offer it. He just stares at me, and I can see the decision forming before he even speaks.

"You're not going to the festival tomorrow night."

The words land like a slap. I blink. "Excuse me?"

"I want you in my house, under guard."

I stare at him. "You can't be serious."

"You'll be safest there. I don't know what's coming, but I know I don't want you in the middle of a crowd. Not at night. Not when anyone or *anything* could be moving through the village. Something terrible could happen."

I cross my arms. "So you're just going to lock me up?"

"It's not like that."

"It feels *exactly* like that." My voice rises without meaning to. "You're doing the same thing my mother did. Hiding me away like I'm fragile. Like I'm not capable of standing on my own."

His jaw tenses. "This isn't about control, Roxy. It's about safety."

"No, it's about fear. *Your* fear."

"Damn right I'm afraid! Do you know how many warriors and hunters we've lost this year Roxy? Dozens! They keep disappearing!" he snaps. "I wasn't just looking for Silas when I found you. I was looking for all of them. You have no idea what could be out there. If something happened to you—"

I step back. "I'm so sorry, Leo. If my being here is putting you in more danger... I don't want to stay."

He looks at me with tears in his eyes. "You being here is worth any potential danger, but I refuse to take your safety for granted. It's just one night," he says, softer now. "I want to protect you."

"And that night?" I ask, voice cracking a little. "It's my *birthday*, Leo."

That stops him cold. He goes still, like someone froze him mid-step. "What?"

"Tomorrow," I whisper. "The festival is on my birthday."

His eyes search mine, and whatever walls he built up in the woods start to fall. Slowly, his shoulders drop. The tension in his hands eases. "I didn't know."

"I wasn't going to say anything," I murmur. "But I was looking forward to it. Just… the music. The dancing. One good memory."

Leo takes a step toward me, and this time, when he speaks, his voice is low, rough, and aching. "You can go, but only if you stay with me. The *entire* night. No wandering off. No slipping into the crowd. I want you where I can see you."

I swallow the lump in my throat. "I promise."

He nods once then again like he's convincing himself. When he pulls me into his arms, I feel the tremble he's trying to hide.

THE DECISION OF THE COUNCIL

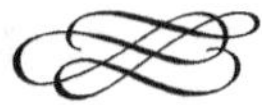

Leo

THE AIR INSIDE THE OLD OUTBUILDING IS DAMP AND COLD, BUT IT'S THE only place on Marek's land where we can be certain no one overhears anything they shouldn't.

I light the lantern on the central table, the flame making shadows on the rough stone walls. Marek shuts the door behind us and bolts it. No one knows we're here.

The silence stretches between us like a taut wire until Marek finally mutters, "We should've seen it coming."

My jaw tightens. "We always do." I grip the edge of the table, trying to will the memory into something more coherent, more explainable, to no avail. "We were halfway down the ridge," I say, my voice low. "And then… something changed. Did you feel it?"

Marek nods, slowly. "Like the air thinned. Like I was holding my breath."

"The birds went quiet first. Then the wind stopped, and I couldn't smell anything. I could barely breathe."

"Everything was still," Marek finishes. "It was like I couldn't hear anything."

I exhale through my nose, the tension building again behind my eyes. "I tried to catch the scent ahead of us and I got nothing. No trace. Like my senses had turned to mud."

"The same thing happened to me," Marek says. "It was like someone poured hot wax over everything we rely on. And then…"

He trails off, but I don't need him to finish. I see it clearly as if it's still happening.

The fog.

Thick. Heavy. Unnatural. It didn't roll in from the river or drift down from the hills—it was just there. In seconds, we were blind, the world swallowed in swirling deep, dark gray.

And then the rogues hit us.

They came fast, soundless at first, then snarling and savage. But they weren't exactly wild. They moved in formation and knew where to strike. Flanks first. Try to split us. Isolate us.

"Harla was ten feet from me," Marek says quietly. "I turned my back for half a second—half a second—and when I turned around, she was gone."

I clench my fists.

"I howled for her. Nothing. No scent, no trail. Just fog and silence."

"And Corwin?" I ask.

He shakes his head. "One moment he was behind me. The next, nothing. Like the fog swallowed him whole."

It's the same every time. Dozens of *my* wolves who never make it back.

"There's something out there," I say. "Something hunting. Something planning. This isn't a string of bad luck. This is deliberate."

Marek's face is stoic in the lantern light, but I see the glint of something there. Fear. "What kind of creature dampens a shifter's senses like that?" he finally asks. "I couldn't even hear my own heartbeat in that fog."

"I don't know," I answer. "But it's not just in our territory. We've heard the rumors—quiet calls for aid from neighboring packs. Missing warriors. Settlements losing numbers."

"Then it's spreading."

I nod grimly. "Which means we need to act now. No more patrols that far out. No more sending small groups into the woods. We don't know what we're facing, and I'm not letting it pick us off one by one."

Marek paces, his boots crunching over the dirt floor. "The council?"

"Tonight," I say. "Quietly. Core elders only. And the warriors we most trust."

"We tell them everything?"

I nod once. "Everything."

He stops pacing. "And what do we call this?"

I look him in the eye.

"A threat," I say. "And one we're already behind on."

MOONSTONE HALL SITS LIKE A SENTINEL ON THE HILLTOP, ITS STONE walls aged with time but crowned in beauty. Set into the outer archways and lining the curved eaves are hundreds of polished moonstones glistening in soft hues of silver, lavender, pale blue, and pearly white. In the daylight, they shimmer like water touched by sunlight. But at night, under the gaze of the moon, they glow faintly from within, casting light across the courtyard. It's said the hall was blessed by the Moon Goddess Herself, and the stones still hum with ancient magic, quiet, steady, and protective.

The high arched ceiling is strung with silver threads that shimmer faintly in the torchlight, and the crescent-shaped hearth at the far end glows with sacred blue flame, lit only during gatherings like this.

The room is full of elders in ceremonial robes and warriors in leather and dark wool. The council is seated. Every face turns toward me, their Alpha.

I step forward, the weight of the day still in my chest, and raise my voice. "This morning," I begin, "Marek and I led a scouting party east of the ridge."

There's no movement, just quiet anticipation. I let the silence stretch a moment, then speak again.

"We were ambushed."

A murmur ripples through the chamber.

"We didn't see it coming," I say. "Didn't smell it. Didn't hear a damn thing until it was too late. Our senses were dulled. Muffled. Like someone poured evil magic into our bones and thickened the air. Then came the fog. And in the fog were rogues, but somehow they were organized. Swift. Waiting for us like they knew the route. We fought them off, but in the chaos, Corwin and Harla disappeared."

The murmurs rise again, louder this time.

"How do you know they were rogues?"

"They are malnourished and lack any noble markings," I say, my voice low. "They were feral, and something felt off about them. Like they belonged nowhere and to no one. They seemed wounded and like there was something rotting beneath their skin. Rogues carry rage, yes, but these had something else clinging to them. Something dark. And the way they moved was organized, too coordinated for true ferals. They didn't fight to survive. They fought to take."

I pause, my jaw tightening.

"And when it was over… not one body was left behind. Just claw marks in the dirt, blood droplets on the leaves, and the stench of black magic. That's how I know. No other trace. No scent trail. Just like with Silas. Just like the others. Gone. Taken."

I look to the elders. "Whatever this is, it isn't random. Something unnatural is moving through our territory. Something that hunts in silence, cloaks its approach in terrible magic, and leaves nothing behind."

There's a tense moment as everyone absorbs the implications, and then I take the next step.

"I believe it may be connected to the witches."

A low buzz spreads like wildfire through the room, paired with startled glances and whispered curses.

"I know some of you have heard the stories," I continue. "Of the child stolen from the Alpha and Luna of Golden Elm Pack twenty-one years ago–a baby taken from her parents by a coven."

Gasps ripple across the crowd.

"Some of you have seen her already. A beautiful young woman with long golden hair, staying at Marek and Hanna's home."

Now voices truly rise. I don't stop them. I let the realization work its way through them like a rising tide.

"I believe Roxy is that child," I say clearly. "The one the coven took."

One of my finest generals stands. "Then she needs to be returned to Golden Elm. Let them deal with what's been done."

Dozens of others murmur their agreement. The atmosphere grows heated, fracturing.

But I hold up a hand.

"I agree that Golden Elm must be involved. But not as our scapegoat. Rather, as our ally."

Silence falls again, wary this time.

"We've all heard whispers of the witches growing bolder. Of towns going dark. Of wolves never returning from patrol. We've all lost something—or someone. This isn't a problem for just one pack."

I sweep the room with my gaze.

"It's time we stop reacting. It's time we fight back. Together. Not as Moon River and Golden Elm and the other pack names we carry—but as one."

I let the words settle.

"We call a summit. We bring the strongest warriors, the best trackers, every elder with even a sliver of knowledge about old magic. And we find that coven. We end this, once and for all."

A long pause follows. Then murmurs again—but this time, they're different.

Urgent. United. Pieces are falling into place.

Finally, Elder Lorna rises. Her silver hair is braided and decorated with moonbeads. Her gaze is as sharp as ever. "The last time our pack dealt with witchcraft and black magic was during the Shadowed

Years. We lost more wolves then than in any war. If it happens again… we cannot face them divided." She turns to me. "I'll support your call, Alpha."

One by one, the others nod in agreement. Marek exhales beside me. It has begun.

The meeting stretches late into the night, the sacred blue flame burning low by the time the final plans are made. My voice is hoarse, my muscles tight, but something inside me settles. The silence afterward is heavy, but it's the silence of resolution, not hesitation.

Elder Lorna folds her hands before her. "Then it's agreed. The day after the festival, our warriors and the Golden Princess will travel to Golden Elm."

"They'll want proof," someone murmurs.

"She is the proof," I say. "They'll know her."

Marek nods beside me. "The baby's hair was so long and bright gold…. They'll know her the moment they lay eyes on her."

"She deserves to meet the family that lost her, and they deserve to know she's alive." I add.

There's a soft ripple of agreement around the chamber.

"It will be a delicate meeting," says a warrior from the back. "They might not welcome outsiders marching in with long-buried truths."

"I'm not marching in with anything," I say. "We're coming with respect. With unity in mind."

Marek leans in. "They'll want to strike back as much as we do. Their pain is older, but it hasn't faded."

"We give them the truth," I say. "Then we give them a choice."

"After the festival," Lorna confirms. "Let us have that night. Let her have it. One night of joy before everything changes."

I swallow hard at that. There's a truth in her words I don't want to face.

Because it *will* change. Once Roxy knows who she is, who she was taken from, she won't be mine to protect, not like she is now. She'll belong to a family. A legacy. A history I can't compete with.

But this isn't about me. It never was.

I step back from the fire, the council's voices already rising behind me in plans and speculation. Marek follows.

We walk out into the cool night. The sky is scattered with stars, and the faintest edge of the moon glows above the trees. Almost full.

We are quiet for a beat. Then he speaks. "You care for her."

It's not a question. I don't answer right away. I just keep walking. "I do," I say finally. "More than I should."

Marek doesn't respond, but his silence isn't judgmental. He knows. He's seen it.

"I just want her to be safe," I murmur. "I want her to have a choice. Not to be handed off or hunted. After the festival," I repeat, more to myself than anyone, "then we go to Golden Elm."

"Then we change everything," Marek says.

And we step back into the light.

The moon is high by the time Marek and I reach the grove.

It lies well beyond the edge of the village, past the outer fields, tucked behind an overgrown ridge where the trees grow thick and gnarled. No one comes here casually. The path is old, nearly forgotten, but I know every twist of it by memory, taught to me in quiet ceremony when I turned seventeen, and my father first whispered the secrets of the Moon River bloodline.

We reach the standing stones just as the wind shifts.

Five granite pillars encircle a sunken hollow, carved with old runes that glow faintly in the moonlight. In the center, half-buried in moss and earth, sits the altar, a slab of silver-veined stone that's older than the village itself.

Only the Alpha may touch it.

Marek steps back. He knows.

I kneel and press my palm to the cold surface. "By blood, by bond, by moon's light," I murmur. The words awaken something beneath the stone, a soft pulse, like the heartbeat of the earth itself.

With a slow groan, the altar shifts. The center opens like a sealed bloom, revealing a hollow lined with velvet, still dry after all these years. Inside are relics of my family. A dagger forged in silverfire. A vial of starlight spring water. My grandfather's oath pendant. Gems, jewels, gold and silver.

And a small, carved box.

I lift it gently. The box is hewn from obsidian and deer antler, and the clasp is shaped like a crescent moon. Inside, nestled in black silk, is the ring.

Moonstone, veined with opal fire, set in a silver band carved with protective sigils. My great-grandmother wore it. Then my grand-mother and mother. It's been passed down, always to the woman who stood beside the Alpha—not just as a mate, but as a protector of the pack's heart. A Luna.

Marek steps closer. "Is that what I think it is?"

I nod, staring down at the stone as it catches the moonlight and glows.

"You're giving it to her?"

"It's hers," I say quietly. "She's not just a lost heir or a witch's stolen prize. She's *Roxy.* Wild, brave, beautiful, and kind."

Marek watches me for a long moment then nods once. "She's going to know how much this means. She'll feel it."

I close the box carefully and tuck it inside the leather satchel I brought. The altar seals behind me with a low sigh, like the stones themselves are breathing again.

As we walk back toward the village, the sky begins to pale in the east—dawn not far off.

Today is the full moon and Roxy's birthday. I don't know what will happen after that. If we'll face war. If she'll leave…. At least I can give her this one night.

One night. One bond. One ring she can wear as a reminder of a promise.

THE GIRL WITH THE HAPPY BIRTHDAY

Roxy

THE SCENT OF BUBBLING BERRY COBBLER FILLS THE KITCHEN, SWEET and sharp. Hanna hums quietly as she carefully folds the last edge of pastry into place. Her curls are pinned up already, copper strands shining in the afternoon light that filters through the window. I stand beside her wearing an apron, my cheeks dusted with flour, doing my best not to burn the crust on our third tray.

"Careful with that one," Hanna says, nudging my side with her elbow. "That's the one we're setting out first. It needs to be pretty."

I glance down at the berries tucked beneath the crust. "No pressure or anything."

She grins. "No pressure. Just the entire pack judging your baking skills on your twenty-first birthday."

I laugh then catch myself. "It's still strange," I say softly. "Being excited. I didn't think I'd feel like this."

"Like what?"

"Safe. Celebrated." I glance at her. "Happy."

Hanna's eyes soften. "You deserve all three."

We leave the cobblers to cool and head to the bedroom where our dresses hang from the wardrobe, the delicate fabric catching the light like water. Mine is a deep midnight blue, simple in shape but edged in silver embroidery, with tiny moons. Hanna's is forest green. It suits her perfectly.

My palms are sweaty as I get dressed and run my fingers down the fabric. "Do I look ridiculous in this?"

Hanna tosses me a look. "You look enchanting. Now stop stalling and sit so I can do your hair."

She pulls a stool to the mirror, and I perch on it, trying not to fidget. Hanna moves behind me with practiced ease, her fingers weaving sections of my hair into an elegant half-braid, letting the rest fall in long loose waves.

"There," she says a few minutes later. "One Goddess-worthy birthday braid."

I lean in close to the mirror. "How'd you do that so fast?"

"Witchcraft," she deadpans.

I snort then swipe a little shimmer on my cheeks and lips.

We finish getting ready as the last light of afternoon fades behind the trees. Outside, the air is cooler, and the music drifts in from the village center.

Hanna steps back, giving me one last once-over. "You ready?"

I exhale slowly. "As I'll ever be."

Then there's a knock on the door.

Hanna winks at me. "I'll get it."

She slips out of the room, and I hear her open the front door. Then her voice floats back, playful and teasing. "Come on in, Alpha. She's just about ready."

I turn as Leo steps into the room.

He's not in armor or leathers tonight. Instead, he wears a deep gray tunic embroidered with silver at the cuffs and a dark blue cloak fastened at his shoulder with a pale blue moonstone pin. His hair is brushed back, and the way he looks at me—

He stops just inside the doorway. His eyes roam over me slowly, reverently, and when they meet mine again, they've darkened. "Happy birthday," he says, his voice low and warm. "You look...." He trails off, shakes his head like he can't find the word. "Stunning doesn't even come close."

My cheeks burn, but I can't stop smiling. "Thank you. You don't look too bad yourself."

He steps closer and reaches for my hand. "Ready to go?"

I glance at Hanna, who gives me a subtle wink before disappearing into the kitchen again, pretending to be very busy cleaning up after the cobblers.

I lace my fingers through Leo's. "Yes. I'm ready."

As we step outside together, dusk is falling, and the festival lights flicker in the distance, music floating like magic through the air. The sky above us is streaked with lavender and pink, the moon already rising behind the pines, full and glowing.

For the first time in a long time, I feel like I belong exactly where I am. Tonight will be a night worth remembering forever.

The village center shines like something out of a dream. Lanterns strung through the trees cast warm golden light over the gathering crowd. The fire pits crackle, casting flickers of orange across faces I've come to recognize, people who were strangers not long ago, now smiling at me like I belong here. Tables overflow with food: roasted meat, spiced vegetables, thick slices of honey-drizzled bread, and of course, the cobblers Hanna and I baked.

The music is alive, fiddles, drums, and pipes weaving together in a rhythm that makes the ground seem to pulse beneath my feet. Children race between the tents, their laughter contagious. A few people shift into their wolf forms and tumble across the grass in a blur of fur and joy.

Leo doesn't leave my side. He keeps his hand lightly on the small of my back, guiding me through the crowd like he thinks I'll float away if he doesn't tether me. He introduces me to people I haven't met yet—elders with wise eyes, warriors with warm smiles, teenagers who shyly wish me happy birthday when Leo tells them what the day is.

He hands me a wooden cup of sweet red wine.

I sip it and grin. "Mmm. Oh my, that's dangerously good."

He laughs under his breath. "Careful," he teases.

We make our way toward the bonfire, which has grown high now, the wood spitting sparks into the sky. People are already dancing barefoot in the grass—couples spinning, friends laughing, older folks clapping along to the beat.

I'm halfway through a bowl of thick venison stew with root vegetables when Hanna appears at my side. "You have to try this." She presses a flask into my hands. "Marek's secret stash."

"Is it safe?"

"Of course," she says, grinning. "It's ale. Strong. Spiced. Amazing."

I take a cautious sip. It's warm, a little sweet, slightly bitter, and tastes like something brewed with magic.

"It's delightful!"

She beams. "Told you."

We end up dancing together next, laughing as we twirl and stomp in time with the music. She spins me under her arm, and I almost fall over, but neither of us care. There's no pressure, no judgment, only joy.

When Leo pulls me into a slower circle, I'm flushed and breathless, my braid coming loose, my face sore from smiling.

"It's like you've lived here your whole life," he murmurs, swaying with me as the rhythm changes to something gentler, more soulful.

"Tonight, I feel like I have."

The moon is full overhead now, bathing the clearing in silver. The music floats on the night air like a promise. Around us, people shift— fur rippling in the firelight, wolves trotting through the edge of the trees, howling once or twice in celebration. There's no fear tonight. No threat. Just community. Pack.

Leo's hands are warm around my waist. I look up at him, and his expression is softer than I've ever seen it. Reverent.

"This is the happiest I've ever seen you," he says.

"It's the happiest I've ever been," I admit, the words slipping out before I can second-guess them.

He brushes a strand of hair from my cheek. "Then I've already done my job."

I smile. "Which is?"

"Making sure you have one perfect birthday."

"You're succeeding."

The next song begins, fast and powerful, and someone from the village tugs Leo away for a quick, laughing dance. I end up with one of the older women who insists she used to win dance competitions "before her knees betrayed her." We laugh, clap, and stomp, and I nearly trip trying to match her pace.

Eventually, I find my way back to Leo. He wraps an arm around my shoulders and pulls me close as we watch the fire burn higher, the music swelling again.

"You're not tired yet?" he asks.

I shake my head. "Are you kidding? I never want this to end."

His gaze lingers on me for a moment, something unreadable in his eyes, but then he just presses a kiss to my temple.

"Then let's make it last," he whispers, "as long as we can."

And under the silver moon, with music in the air and joy like wildfire in my chest, I feel like tonight, I am exactly where I'm meant to be.

The music fades behind us as we slip into the trees, hand in hand.

Leo doesn't say where we're going. He just glances at me every so often, that quiet smile playing at the corner of his lips. It's the kind of smile that makes my heart skip even though I pretend it doesn't.

The forest is silver with moonlight, every leaf brushed with a quiet kind of magic. I hear laughter echoing from the festival grounds, but it's distant now, like a memory already drifting away. Out here, it's just us and the hush of branches swaying. Leo's hand is warm and strong around mine.

"Where are we going?" I whisper.

He squeezes my fingers. "Somewhere special. Just for tonight."

We crest the hill, and tucked between two ancient pines, I see a stone structure half-hidden by ivy. It looks like it grew from the earth itself. The walls are pale gray and shimmering faintly in the dark, inlaid with veins of what I think might be moonstone, glowing softly beneath the surface. A round tower rises at the back, and over the arched doorway is a carved crescent moon so worn with time that it looks like it's been kissed by centuries of weather and worship.

Leo pushes open the heavy wooden door, and a breath of warm, cedar-scented air rushes out to meet us.

Inside, it's quiet and glowing. Hundreds of tiny crystal orbs hang suspended from the ceiling like captured stars, casting flickering light across the stone floor. Tapestries cover the curved walls, woven in silver thread with images of the moon in its many phases, wolves mid-shift, and swirling starlight and magic. A small fountain gurgles near the center of the room, its water catching the light like liquid diamonds.

I turn in a slow circle, staring, my breath catching in my throat. "Leo... what is this place?"

He steps beside me, his voice low. "It's called the Crescent Heart. Built by our ancestors, blessed by the Goddess. My pack has guarded it for generations. No one comes here lightly."

I turn in place again, my eyes wide, my heart thudding in my chest. "Why did you bring me here?"

Leo watches me for a long moment. His expression shifts, gentling, like something deep inside him is unfolding. "Because tonight is important. And so are you."

My chest tightens, warmth rising up through my ribs and into my throat.

He steps closer. "I need to tell you something. Before the festival ends. Before everything changes."

My heart begins to race again, but not from dancing this time.

His gaze doesn't waver. "Tomorrow, I'm taking you to Golden Elm."

The breath catches in my lungs. "What? Why?"

"You're the child they lost. The one taken from their Alpha and Luna all those years ago."

I blink. My mind is spinning. "But... how do you know for sure?"

"I don't," he admits. "Not yet, but everything points to it. And they deserve to see you. You deserve to meet them. I'm not letting this secret stay buried, not when it could change everything for you. You have the right to know who you are. Where you came from."

I don't realize I'm crying until he brushes a tear from my cheek with his thumb. "You're taking me there," I whisper. "Yourself?"

He nods. "My strongest warriors and me. For your safety. But also…" He looks out over the glowing flowers. "I'm going to ask Golden Elm to join us in this fight against the witches. We can't do this alone anymore. Not with what we're facing."

I press a hand to my mouth, overwhelmed. The firelight still burns on my skin, and the taste of wine lingers on my tongue, but this moment—this moment is entirely different. He's offering me something no one ever has before.

Answers. Family. A future.

"I don't even know what to say," I whisper. "Thank you. Leo, thank you for… everything. You've saved me more than once, and you keep giving me reasons to believe I'm not just a burden."

He shakes his head, stepping close again. "You're not a burden, Roxy. This is the beginning of something bigger than either of us can see."

I throw my arms around him before I can stop myself. He holds me like I'm something precious. Like I'm not broken. Like I'm worth all this effort.

When I finally pull back, his hand lingers on my waist. His other hand tilts my chin gently upward. "Happy birthday," he murmurs.

And then, at last, he kisses me.

His lips are warm and sure and full of everything he hasn't said out loud. I kiss him back like I've been waiting for this moment my whole life—because I have been.

THE MATE BOND WITH THE ALPHA

My lips are still tingling.

I can feel the heat of Leo's hands on my waist, and my heart thuds so hard I think it might echo in the stillness of the sacred space around us.

He pulls back just enough to look at me, and there's something in his expression I haven't seen before.

"I was going to wait until tomorrow to tell you," he says quietly, his thumb brushing against my cheek. "Let you have the festival and your birthday without anything hanging over your head."

I blink up at him, still breathless. "You mean about going to Golden Elm?"

"Yes, about Golden Elm." He swallows, like the words are heavier than they should be. "We're leaving mid-day tomorrow. Marek and I, along with some of my best warriors. We will be escorting you there."

For a second, I can't breathe. Tomorrow? My mind races, a thousand questions crashing through me, none of them quite forming words. And then the reality lands—*he's giving this to me.* A chance I never thought I'd get.

"You did this for me?" I whisper.

"I had to," he says. "Not just because of who you are… but because of what I feel when I'm with you. I wanted you to know before I gave you this."

He reaches into his cloak and pulls out a small, carved wooden box. It's smooth and polished, the lid etched with a crescent moon.

I stare at it, my heart thudding. "What is it?"

Leo opens it slowly, and nestled in black velvet is the most beautiful ring I've ever seen.

The moonstone is veined with opal fire, a swirl of pale blue and soft violet that seems to pulse faintly in the low light. It's set in a silver band carved with tiny protective sigils, ancient ones, curling like vines around the stone. It glows in the stillness—like it *knows* it belongs to the moon.

"I don't expect anything from you," Leo says, gently taking the ring from its box. "This isn't a bond mark. It's not a claim."

"Then… what is it?" I ask, my voice barely above a whisper.

"It's a promise," he says simply. "That I will protect you, no matter what comes. That I'll stand beside you when you face whatever truths are waiting in Golden Elm. That even if everything changes tomorrow, you'll never be alone."

My eyes sting. No one has ever given me anything like this before.

I hold out my hand, and he slides the ring onto my finger. It fits perfectly, like it was made for me. The stone gleams in the lantern light of the Crescent Heart, casting pale reflections on the floor.

"It was my mother's," Leo says quietly. "And her mother's before her. Every woman who wore it protected something sacred. Now it's yours."

I can't speak. I'm too full of emotion and gratitude. I stare down at the ring then up at Leo.

"You keep doing this," I say softly.

"Doing what?"

"Saving me. Giving me things I didn't even know I needed." I take a shaky breath and lean into him, and he wraps his arms around me.

"Thank you," I murmur. "For this. For everything."

He presses a kiss to the top of my head. "You're worth it."

I stare down at the moonstone once more. It feels warm on my skin. Alive or enchanted somehow. Not just a symbol of the past, but of something still unwritten. A beginning.

And tomorrow... I travel to find the people who lost me.

But tonight, I have this place. This ring. This promise.

And Leo.

There's something about this moment that feels... suspended. Like time's been folded in half and set aside just for us. Everything else—the witches, the missing, the truth waiting in Golden Elm—fades to the edges of my mind.

What remains is him. His steady gaze. The quiet rise and fall of his chest. The warmth of his hands, still cradling mine.

"Leo," I whisper.

He doesn't say anything, just leans in and brushes his lips across mine. It's not a question, not a demand—it's a thread, pulling me closer.

I rise onto my tiptoes and kiss him with everything I'm feeling. Gratitude. Longing. Something deeper, more fragile. He responds in kind, his hand cupping the back of my neck, his fingers tangling in my hair.

The kiss deepens, and I can feel it unraveling something in both of us. The walls we were holding up, whatever hesitation kept us from this moment, crumble.

I curl my hands into his shirt, and he pauses just long enough to search my eyes.

"I want this. I want *you*." I whisper.

His jaw tightens, and I can see how much it means to him. How much he's holding back.

We don't rush.

Leo guides me gently across the floor of Crescent Heart, where the stone is warm beneath our feet and the light from the lanterns casts everything in silvers and golds. He kisses me again, and I feel him inhale sharply when I slide my hands beneath the hem of his shirt.

His skin is hot under my fingers. Solid. Strong.

He helps me ease it over his head, and then I begin to unlace the front of my dress. My fingers tremble slightly, but not from nerves. From the way he's looking at me—like he's awestruck, like I'm his.

Bit by bit, we shed the layers between us. My dress falls, pooling at my feet. He sheds the rest of his clothes. It's not just about lust—it's about closeness. About two people standing in a space that feels like it was made for them.

He leads me to a stack of furs at the edge of the room, and they cradle us like they were meant for this moment too.

Leo hovers over me, his hand splayed against my ribs, just below my heart. I can feel it pounding against his palm.

"I can't promise I know what's coming," he whispers, placing his forehead against mine. "But I'll fight for you. For us."

"I know," I whisper back.

And then he kisses me again.

He slides his hands over my breasts and moves his mouth to my neck. I cry out in pleasure. The world narrows to sensation—the weight of his body on top of mine, the way his fingers explore every inch of me.

His mouth finds a nipple, and each kiss makes my body arch toward his. I feel him at my entrance, and I beg him to claim me.

He presses inside me slowly, inch by inch until he's buried deep within me. We move together, finding a rhythm all our own, wrapped in ecstasy. His name slips from my lips, and he answers with mine, like a vow.

When it's over, we lie tangled together, my head on his chest, his hand stroking slow circles along my spine.

The moonlight streams through the high windows, bathing us in silver, and the ring glows on my finger.

Now I know, whatever happens tomorrow, I'll carry this moment with me forever. Tonight, I wasn't a mystery or a prophecy or a problem to solve.

I was just his. And he was mine.

Something stirs deep inside me.

At first, I think it's just the afterglow of what we shared, and the way he looked at me, but this feels different. A warmth blooms low in my spine and spreads like wildfire through my limbs, igniting everything it touches. It's not painful, but it's powerful, like something locked tight for years is being set free at long last.

I sit up, my breath catching. "Leo…"

He lifts his head immediately, his dark eyes narrowing in concern. "What is it?"

"I… I don't know." I press a hand to my chest. My heart isn't just pounding—it's changing. The rhythm of it, the depth. "I feel… strange. But not in a bad way. Just—different."

Leo sits up beside me, his fingers brushing my cheek. "Your eyes," he whispers. "Roxy… they're glowing."

A low sound rumbles in my throat. Not a cry. Not a scream. A growl.

But it doesn't scare me.

I stand, my legs shaking, and step into the center of Crescent Heart. The silver firelight dances over my bare skin. The ring on my finger pulses with warmth, almost as if it recognizes what's happening.

And then… it begins.

My bones don't break, they *unfold*. My skin shimmers gold before fur spills across it like starlight. My limbs lengthen, reshape, and my vision sharpens. The air bursts with scent, sound, color. Every instinct I never knew I had flares to life.

I fall forward onto four legs, and when I look down, I see paws. Strong, elegant, golden.

I'm a wolf.

I stand there, panting lightly. My heart is pounding in my chest as the final threads of the shift settle into place. My reflection flickers in the polished floor—sleek golden fur, long legs, bright eyes that still carry something human.

Leo stares at me in stunned wonder.

Then, without a word, he shifts.

His form ripples and collapses with practiced grace, and in seconds, the massive midnight-black wolf stands before me. Regal. Fierce. Familiar.

His eyes—Leo's eyes—find mine.

And we run out of Crescent Heart, across the fields, and through the trees.

The night wraps around us like silk as our paws strike the earth in unison. My lungs drink in the clean air, and everything is brighter, sharper, more *alive*. The wind rushes through my fur. The moon above us beams like it was waiting just for this–for us.

We leap over rocks and dip through groves of whispering birch. Leo keeps pace easily, his dark form a shadow beside my light. We don't speak—but we don't need to. Every motion is a conversation. Every glance is understanding.

I'm free.

That's what the shift feels like. Like I was only ever half alive before this night. Like something was buried inside me—something waiting for the moment I was truly seen. Truly loved.

Leo circles me as we reach the meadow beyond the ridge, where wildflowers bloom even in the dark. He brushes his muzzle against mine, and I nuzzle him back. I can feel his pride, his awe, like heat radiating off his skin.

And something deeper.

Mine, his soul seems to say.

I turn my golden face to the sky and howl. It's a sound pulled from deep inside my chest—raw, ancient, and full of wonder. He joins me, and our voices rise together, weaving through the night like a hymn to the Moon Goddess Herself.

This is my birthright. This is my truth.

Not stolen. Not hidden. *Claimed.*

When the howls fade, we lie down in the tall grass, side by side.

Leo presses against me, warm and steady, and I curl into him, my fur brushing his.

Whatever waits at Golden Elm, we'll face it, and I'll finally know who I am.

And I'm not alone.

THE RIDERS AT THE VILLAGE

Leo

The moon hangs low by the time we circle back toward Crescent Heart.

Roxy runs ahead of me, her golden fur catching the silver light in flashes. She's breathtaking like this, wild and radiant–fully herself. Every movement is full of grace and joy. She cuts through the wind like she was born to run beneath the stars.

We slow as the sacred building comes into view, rock and moonstone gleaming in the night. I nudge her gently with my shoulder, and she gives a playful yip before trotting toward the arched entrance.

I shift first. My fur gives way to skin. The shift comes easily tonight, smooth and instinctive. I stretch my arms, roll my shoulders, and grab the folded clothes I stashed behind the ceremonial screen earlier.

Roxy follows suit, her body shimmering as she shifts back into her human form, glorious and gorgeous in the faint moonlight.

We take our time dressing, the silence between us peaceful. It's the kind of quiet that comes when everything has fallen into place.

Once we're ready, I offer her my hand. She takes it, her fingers lacing through mine like it's the most natural thing in the world.

The walk back to my house is slow and calm, the night air crisp against our skin. The village is quiet now, most of the lanterns extinguished, only a few windows glowing with the last flickers of firelight.

When we reach the porch, I unlock the door and guide her inside. The house is warm from the fire I left banked earlier. I light a lamp in the main room, casting golden light across the walls.

"Come on," I say softly. "Let's get some sleep. We have a big day tomorrow."

She nods, stifling a yawn with the back of her hand.

I lead her upstairs to my room, where thick blankets wait on the bed, and the moonlight pours through the windows in soft slivers. I pull back the covers, and she climbs in without hesitation, curling onto her side. I strip off my shirt and slide in beside her.

For a moment, we just lie there, staring at the ceiling, listening to each other breathe.

Then she turns toward me, one hand resting lightly on my chest. "I still don't believe this is real."

"It is," I murmur, brushing a strand of hair from her face. "You shifted, ran, and howled. And tomorrow… we will take you home."

Her eyes search mine. "Do you think they'll recognize me?"

"I think they'll *know* you and love you."

She smiles softly and rests her head against my shoulder, her fingers tracing idly over my ribs. I wrap my arm around her, pulling her close.

"Thank you," she whispers.

"For what?"

"For the ring, the promise, and not letting me remain a prisoner."

There's a lump in my throat, but I just kiss her forehead and hold her tighter.

She drifts off before I do, her breathing evening out, her body warm against mine. I lie there in the dark, my heart still racing from everything we've just shared.

The sky is just beginning to pale at the edges when I wake. Roxy lies beside me, curled into the blankets, her hair a golden spill across the pillow. Her breathing is soft and even, her face peaceful.

I don't move. I just lie there, watching her, memorizing this moment.

And then—

"Leo." Marek's voice cuts through the early morning haze, sharp and insistent. *"You awake?"*

I blink and then respond through the link. *"I am. What is it?"*

"A patrol intercepted riders in the forest—shifters in human form. They claim to be messengers. Meet me at the gates."

I'm already sliding out of bed, careful not to wake Roxy. *"Where are they from?"*

"Ebonlight Pack."

I throw on my clothes, my boots hitting the floor with heavy finality. I pause once at the door, glancing back at Roxy. She's still sleeping soundly, the moonstone ring glowing faintly on her finger.

She doesn't need this right now. Not before everything changes again.

Outside, the morning is crisp and still, the first light of dawn brushing the treetops. I move fast through the village, my stride long and quiet, until I reach the outer gates.

Marek is already there, his arms crossed and brows furrowed. Beside him, two warriors stand alert, flanking three shifters on horseback.

The horses are restless, with sweat on their flanks and foam at the reins. They've been ridden hard. The messengers wear black-and-gray leathers, their cloaks bearing a subtle crest: a raven in flight.

One of them, a tall woman with a scar across her chin, dismounts first.

"Alpha," she says, bowing her head with a warrior's respect, "I am Verona of Ebonlight Pack. This is Monett. We come with news."

I nod once. "Go ahead."

She doesn't mince words. "The Thistle and Boar Inn was ambushed three nights ago."

My stomach drops.

The inn where Roxy and I stayed.

Verona continues. "It was a coven of witches. They were looking for someone. A young woman. They tore the place apart. Killed half the guests—shifters and humans alike."

Marek swears under his breath beside me.

"We arrived after the attack," Monett says. "We tried to track them, but magic—dark magic—obscured their trail. The inn's gone, burned to the ground. The survivors say the witches kept asking about a girl with golden hair and sapphire eyes."

I clench my jaw. I knew they'd be looking for her.

Verona lowers her voice. "We believe your pack is harboring the one they're after, but we aren't here to expose her. We're here to offer help."

I glance at Marek and then back at her. "You're certain about that?"

Verona nods once. "Our Alpha sends us with this message: Ebonlight Pack does not bow to dark forces. We've seen what the coven is doing, the death and disappearances they've left in their wake. We want to join Moon River as allies, not just in words but in war."

I exhale slowly. This is bigger than we feared, but at least we're not alone. "You came at the right time," I say. "We're riding to Golden Elm today with the young woman."

Her eyes flicker with realization. "She's the stolen child?"

I nod. "We believe so. We're going to offer Golden Elm the same thing you just offered us. A united front."

The Ebonlight messengers' expressions sharpen with approval. Monett speaks. "Then we stand with you, and we'll ride into battle when called."

Marek steps forward. "For now, rest. Eat. Let your horses recover. We'll prepare for our journey, and when the time comes, you'll be among the first summoned."

"Thank you," Verona says and bows again. "We'll be ready."

"The witches are already circling," I reply. "They're done hiding."

I glance toward the village, where smoke begins to rise from the morning hearths, and the sun breaks fully over the horizon.

Today, everything changes.

Again.

THE THREAT IN THE FOG

Roxy

THE MIDDAY LIGHT SLIPS IN THROUGH THE CURTAINS, GOLDEN AND SOFT against the wooden floor. I stir beneath the covers, warm and wrapped in Leo's scent. For a moment, I let myself stay there, tucked in the cocoon of his bed and the magic of last night.

But then his hand brushes against my cheek, his voice rumbling low beside me. "Roxy, it's time."

I blink slowly, still somewhere between sleep and waking. His face is close, his eyes darker than ever in the shadows. My heart flutters. "Already?" I whisper, stretching under the covers.

He nods, brushing a lock of hair from my face. "It's past noon. The others are readying the horses. The warriors will ride rather than making the journey in wolf form so we can greet your family appropriately and make a formal appearance. I let you sleep in as long as I could."

Last night floods back to me—his kiss, making love, the sacred ring on my finger, the shift. My very first shift.

Once I dress and our bags are packed, we step out into the sunlight, and I squint against the brightness.

Down in the courtyard, dozens of warriors are already in position and waiting, most of them dressed in armor, dark leather, their weapons strapped across their backs. Marek is there, too, adjusting his saddle straps.

Hanna stands next to him. "Don't forget to eat while you're gone," she says, handing me a basket of food.

I smile and wrap my arms around her. "Thank you for everything."

She hugs me tight. "You've got a whole life waiting for you now, but don't forget about me. You'll always have a place here."

Nodding, I squeeze her shoulder. "I could never forget about you. See you soon." I take a step away and give her a little wave.

Marek steps forward and kisses Hanna goodbye. "We'll be back before too long–with good news, I hope."

"You'd better," she replies, trying to sound stern but failing. "I'll be waiting."

Leo approaches her last, and she grabs his arm.

"Take care of her," she says quietly. "She's strong, but she's new to all this."

He nods solemnly. "I know. I won't let anything happen to her."

I feel the heat rise in my chest at their concern. They're risking an awful lot just to take me home.

Leo helps me mount the dappled mare they've chosen for me. She's tall and sure-footed, with soft eyes and a steady gait. I grip the reins, nerves and excitement twining through me like ivy.

Leo swings up onto his horse, a powerful black stallion that seems almost too perfectly matched to him. Marek rides beside him, issuing quiet orders to the warriors who fan out to either side of us in protective formation.

We ride out through the village, and people gather in doorways and along the main road. Some nod in respect. Others call out quiet wishes for safe travels. A few children wave, and I wave back, smiling despite the knot in my stomach.

As we pass over the river bridge that marks the edge of Moon

River territory, I glance back one last time at the village. I'm leaving it to chase a journey that's waited over two decades to find me. It seems surreal.

"You okay?" Leo asks, his voice low beside me.

I turn back toward the road. "Yes," I say softly. "I think I'm ready."

"No matter what happens, I'll be with you."

I look at him, and something in me settles. The road ahead might be uncertain, but with Leo beside me, and the ring still warm on my finger, I don't feel lost. I feel like I'm finally going home.

We ride through the towering trees, the horses' hooves muffled by the soft earth and birdsong overhead. Leo rides beside me, his posture alert. His dark eyes scan the trail ahead. Marek brings up the rear, surrounded by fifty Moon River warriors on horseback. They're strong. Loyal. A moving wall of muscle and steel.

I should feel safe, but something is wrong. A sudden chill rolls in, sliding over my skin like icy breath. The sunlight vanishes.

Fog. It pours in from nowhere, heavy and unnatural, blanketing the path, the trees, even the sky. It's as thick as wool and dark gray. I blink, trying to see Leo, but his features are already fading.

"Leo?" My voice sounds distant–hollow.

He doesn't answer.

The fog presses in from all sides, swallowing up the world. A prickle of dread blooms in my gut.

Marek growls low behind me. "Something's wrong. I can't scent anything."

I hear Leo finally. "I can barely see or hear you! Roxy?"

The horses start to panic, their hooves stamping and ears twitching, their nostrils flaring at ghosts in the fog. The warriors murmur among themselves.

No sound. No scent. No sight.

And then—

Mother.

She materializes through the mist like a nightmare on a dark horse with eyes like glowing coals. But, she looks different–older–but not just in the lines etched across her face or the graying of her hair.

No, there's something deeper, some sort of rotting under her gap-toothed smile.

"Hello, little one." Her voice slithers through the silence like a snake.

Behind her I spot a group of wolves. They look like the rogues we saw in the meadow, the ones Leo protected me from. All of them look exactly the same. Their bodies are unnaturally thin, with pale gray coats and bloodshot eyes. They block the path.

My hands tremble on the reins.

Leo says, angrily, "Get behind me, Roxy."

Marek shifts fully, his fur bristling, his claws digging into the earth.

But it's already too late.

The witch who claimed to be my mother lifts one bony hand, her fingers trailing sparks of sickly green light. I feel it hit me before I can even scream. It's like falling in a sea full of ice. My body goes rigid. I can't move. My arms and legs are frozen solid, as is my mouth. The reins slip from my fingers. My horse rears, and I tumble from the saddle like a rag doll.

"Roxy!" Leo dives for me—he's a blur of movement—but the rogues charge in.

One of them slams into him mid-air, dragging him down in a chaos of snarls and limbs.

The warriors are shifting, too, their wolves emerging in flashes of fur and fury. Claws meet claws. Fangs clash with fangs. But there are so many rouges—more than we saw at first. They seem to pour in from the fog itself.

I lie helpless, frozen on the forest floor. I can't blink, cry out, or even twitch.

A dozen more witches step in from the mist like phantoms, wearing long cloaks trailing through the mud, their hands raised and glowing. They chant in a language I don't understand.

One of them lifts me with a flick of her hand, like I weigh nothing. My body floats, limp and useless. I want to scream. I want to fight. But I can barely even *breathe.*

The witch I once called Mother watches it all with a quiet smile. "Did you really think you could outrun me forever?" she whispers.

I'm slung across the back of her horse like cargo. My cheek presses into the rough leather of the saddle, and the world tilts as we start to move.

Behind me, Leo howls. The sound shatters something in my chest. He sees them taking me, but he's trapped, surrounded. He can't reach me.

They ride through the fog without fear, the witches fanning out around us like shadows on horseback. The mist swallows the sounds of the battle behind us until even Leo's howl is gone.

I can't move, or cry. But I can *feel.* Terror, rage, and heartbreak pulse through me.

The witch strokes my hair as we ride. "There, there, little one. We're going home."

And I can do nothing but watch as everything I love disappears behind a curtain of fog. The trees blur past as the witches fly. We're no longer galloping. We are actually *flying.*

Their horses don't touch the ground. They hover just above it, their hooves skimming the earth without a sound, trailing mist in their wake. The wind bites at my skin, sharp as needles, but I can't even shiver. My limbs are still frozen. My tongue is a stone in my mouth. I'm not even sure if my heart is still beating normally or if it's just the rush of terror filling my ears.

I'm slung belly-down over the saddle like a sack of grain, jostling with every unnatural turn of the horse beneath me. My face slams against the leather, but I can't lift my head.

I *feel* every sickening lurch, every gust of freezing wind. Every moment takes me farther and farther from Leo. I reach for him in the only way I still can.

"Leo," I try through the mind-link. *"Leo, please—can you hear me?"*

The response is empty silence–nothing–as if he's too far, or—

No. No, I won't think that. But the fear is there, gnawing at me, louder than reason.

What if he's dead?

What if those wolves tore him apart before he could shift? What if he fell trying to protect me? What if I never see him again, never hear his laugh, never feel the weight of his gaze, never get to tell him what's been burning in my chest since the day we met?

I squeeze my eyes shut, and even that feels like too much effort.

"Please, Leo. Please find me. Please be alive."

Still nothing.

The witch behind me moves in her saddle, adjusting her grip. I feel her bony fingers in my hair, smoothing it back with mock affection. "You can stop trying," she says coldly. "No one's coming." Her voice drips with satisfaction, like she can feel my panic and wants to taste it. "You've been playing in the light too long, little girl," she murmurs. "But you were *mine* first."

I want to spit in her face and scream at her, to tear free of whatever spell she's wrapped me in and run back to Leo, but my body won't obey. My wolf is silent–caged. Whatever magic they've used, it's not just paralyzing my limbs. It's severing the part of me that fights, that protects, that runs.

I can't shift.

Even when I reach inward, clawing at the space where my wolf usually prowls, it's empty, like she's been locked in a box and buried deep. I feel hollow, trapped in my own skin.

The forest thickens around us, but the witches don't slow. They fly between trunks with eerie ease, their cloaks whipping like wings. Some of them start to chant again, low and guttural, the sound vibrating through the air like the hum of insects.

I try to track how far we've come, but it's hopeless. I think about the others–Marek and the warriors. My heart lurches at the thought of Hanna, of the warriors' mates back at Moon River. What will they think when they realize their mates are gone?

And their pain is all my fault....

The witch leans closer. I can feel her breath against my ear. "You don't belong with them." Her voice is sharp as a blade wrapped in silk. "You're not one of them. You were *born* for us. You'll remember that soon." She laughs, and it's a sound that makes my skin crawl. "I'll take such good care of you, just like I always have."

I clench my jaw. Inside, I scream. She didn't care for me. She *used* me. She *hurt* me. And I'll never forget that, even if I'm paralyzed and powerless.

Somewhere deep in my chest, beneath the fear, the silence, and the spell that holds me, I make a promise.

I will not stay her prisoner, and I will *never* forget who I am.

THE ROGUES IN THE FOG

Leo

Fog clings to everything, and I can't see more than a few feet ahead.

"Roxy!"

Her name rips out of me as she tumbles from her horse. I launch forward, but I'm too slow. Something slams into me. A rogue. Then another. Then more.

Snarls explode around me. Marek shifts, his silver fur gleaming through the mist. The warriors follow suit, growling, snapping, their claws scraping the earth. The rogues are fast, unhinged, their bodies jerking like puppets. But there aren't many of them—eight, maybe ten at most.

It's not about the numbers. It was *never* about the numbers. The witches sacrificed these rogues to distract us.

I tear one off my shoulder and sink my teeth into its throat. Blood fills my mouth. The thing doesn't even scream, just dies with wide, unblinking eyes. Another one charges, and I rake it down with my claws, my wolf in full control now. I don't have time to savor the kill. I'm fighting like hell to get to her.

"Roxy!" I try through the mind-link.

Nothing.

I whip around and see Roxy, just for a heartbeat. She's limp, draped across a horse like a broken doll. And she's with *her*––the witch.

She's already vanishing back into the trees, surrounded by others in dark cloaks, their horses floating above the ground like shadows torn loose from the earth.

I howl, but the fog swallows the sound whole.

Marek crashes into a rogue beside me, driving it to the ground with a vicious snap of his jaws. Another warrior leaps from above, pinning a snarling rogue into the mud. It's chaos, but we're winning.

One by one, the rogues fall. Their strikes are wild, frantic, lacking the unity of a true pack. They're not here to kill us. They're here to *delay* us.

It's working.

The last rogue lunges at my flank, but I twist mid-air and break its neck with one swipe. It drops in a heap of bone and fur.

The clearing goes silent. The fog lingers. Bodies are strewn across the grass, bloodied and broken. My warriors pant in the mist. A couple are wounded, but all of them are alive.

"They're gone," Marek says. *"They took her."*

I stagger forward to the spot where I last saw her. The earth is torn up from claws, and I see a crushed patch of grass where she fell from her horse. I drop to my knees and press my hand to it. It's still warm.

"Roxy..." I whisper. *"I'm sorry."*

The warriors circle, still in wolf form, blood drying in their fur. They look to me not just for orders, but for hope–for assurance.

"She's alive," Marek says after a moment, quietly. *"She has to be. They need her powers."*

"She couldn't shift," I reply. *"She didn't fight. That spell—whatever they hit her with...."*

Marek meets my eyes. *"They came for her. This whole thing was a distraction."*

They had ten rogue wolves under their control from some sort of spell. But there were dozens of us. They never expected to win. They just needed enough time to steal her.

The bond between us—the one that sang during her shift, that pulsed like a heartbeat the night I claimed her—has gone faint. It's not broken, but it's dulled, like someone's smothered it under layers of stone.

"She's out there," I say louder, through the link, turning to face the warriors. *"We will find her."*

They're ready.

Every second we wait is another second they drag her deeper into the forest.

"The witches did what they came to do. But we are going to make them regret it. Listen carefully. This is what happens next. Twenty of you are heading to Golden Elm. When you reach the high court, ask for the Alpha. Tell him what's happened and that we need their best warriors to meet us in the Moonbeam Valley near where the old Thistle and Boar Inn used to stand. Follow our scent, and we will guide you there."

I turn to the others—the thirty who remain, breathing hard and ready to bleed.

"You cross the Ember Ridge by nightfall and fan out. Some of you head for the Ebonlight Pack lands. Another group head toward the vineyards at Raven Square, and tell the Luna there of our plan to banish the witches from these lands forever. Anyone you find along the way, tell them we fight in the secret Moonbeam Valley at dawn."

The fog begins to lift, but the scent of blood lingers in the air.

The world blurs beneath my paws. Roots, rocks, and wind-split trees rush by as I run faster than I ever have before.

Marek is just behind me, his silver wolf a streak in the underbrush. Our warriors are making their way to the territories they bring messages to, but this? This part—we do alone.

***

We've been running flat out for over an hour, the wind tearing through our fur, the forest whirring by all around us. My lungs burn, but I don't slow, not even when Marek stumbles beside me. When the blackened remains of the Thistle and Boar come into view, I skid to a halt, my heart pounding. It really is gone–just ash and ruin where there used to be warmth and light.

We stand at the edge of the ruins. The old inn is nothing but ash and collapsed beams now. The wooden sign lies broken in the mud, its paint scorched away. Smoke still clings to the wreckage, bitter in the back of my throat.

With no time to waste, we keep running until we get to the cliffs where the trees grow impossibly tall, their trunks pale as bone. The moss grows thicker here, and there should be a wall of vines woven so tightly it looks like the forest ends.

But now… it's gone.

There's no wall. No veil. Just a jagged cliffside covered in tangled brambles and scattered stones. It looks like any other part of the wilds. Unremarkable. Uninviting.

I pace along the cliff, my claws digging into the wet earth. *"It has to be here. A valley doesn't just vanish."*

"If it's enchanted, it can be hidden. Sealed. You know that. That's why so few find it. That's why it's a secret." Marek sniffs at a patch of ground where the vines once hung.

I catch Roxy's scent in the breeze. I can feel her nearby.

"Roxy! Can you hear me?" I try to find her through the mind-link.

Marek prowls the cliff's edge. *"If the witches sealed the entrance, we'll need to break it open. But that kind of spell work? It'll take power."*

I bare my teeth. *"We don't have time for spells and power."*

I push my head through a tangle of dead brush and slam my shoulder against the cliff wall. Stone. Cold and unmoving. It doesn't matter. I do it again.

And again.

I lower my head, breathing hard. My heart is a raw wound in my chest. Every moment that passes is another moment she's away from me. She's scared. I can feel it, even if I can't hear her. She tried to reach me. I *know* she did.

We have to find a way inside.

"She's in there," I say through the mind-link, pacing.

Marek's wolf sits beside me, calm but watchful. *"I caught her scent here, too. Why can't we see the entrance?"*

I lower my head toward the dirt. My chest aches with helplessness.

Moon Goddess, I pray silently, the way my mother taught me as a pup. *You gave her to me. You bound her to my soul. Don't take her away now. Please—show me the way. Open the veil. Let me find her.*

Wind stirs through the trees above, soft and cold. The light around us shifts—dusk bleeding across the sky in shades of violet and charcoal. The first star appears overhead and then another.

Not all at once but in a ripple, like a curtain of water disturbed by a breeze, the vines begin to snake down from the stone—growing, threading together until the outline forms.

A wall of ivy. Thick. Twisting. Alive.

The veil.

"Marek, I see it."

His ears perk up and his tail rises.

"It wasn't gone. It was hidden."

The vines part slowly, revealing a narrow path carved into the mountain. It's a path I've walked twice before.

I blink and it clicks.

"The other times I came here...." I pause, remembering the silver light through the trees, the hush, the sense of stepping into something sacred. *"It was dusk both times. The moon was rising. That's the key."*

"So it's tied to moonlight, and the Moon Goddess," Marek says. *"That means it's old magic. Cyclical. It only reveals itself during transitions."*

I step closer, my heart pounding. The valley glows beyond the veil, stunning and silent, cloaked in flowers and moonlight.

Roxy is in there. I can feel her.

"I'm going in." I stare down the narrow trail, my claws sinking into the mossy earth. *"I need to find her."*

His eyes sharp, Marek moves in front of me. *"Wait. Leo—don't do anything reckless. Only step in if they're hurting her. But if they're not..."*

"I'll wait." I nod. *"I'll stay hidden and watch."*

"Good. Then I'll stay here. I'll show the others the way in."

I meet his gaze, steady and sure. *"Tell them to hide in the cliffs and shadows. I want them tucked into the mountain until dawn. We'll strike with the first light. I'll wait until morning unless they hurt her."*

He nods once and steps aside. The path before me opens–wide and inviting.

Inside the valley, the world shifts. The air is heavier, and the colors are deeper. Magic hums underfoot like a heartbeat. My fur prickles as I move deeper into the trees. My paws are silent on the mossy trail.

I move like a shadow through the trees, keeping to the edges, my wolf sharp and low to the ground. Through the breaks in the branches, I see movement–torches, cloaks, and shapes pacing outside the tower.

The fire crackles in the clearing, painting the trees in flickering orange light. I crouch just beyond its reach, hidden in the dense underbrush, still in my wolf form with my belly low to the ground. The scent of wine and smoke drifts toward me, mingling with the pungent odor of dark magic.

They've made camp like they're on holiday. Thirteen witches, cloaked in silk and smoke, gather around the bonfire. Their horses graze just beyond the ring of trees, untethered. There's no fear here. No urgency. They believe they've won.

One of them tosses her head back and laughs, her dark hair gleaming in the firelight. Another raises a silver goblet and slurs something about how lovely it is to be young forever. They pass a bottle of dark wine between them, dancing barefoot in the dirt, toasting to their own beauty, their power, their cleverness.

A few of them chant in low tones beneath their breath, conjuring spirits out of the smoke. But most just drink, laugh, and talk about their beautiful young faces and bodies.

They don't speak of Roxy. They don't need to. To them, she's already tucked away. Handled. But I see her tower rising high behind them. The window is dark.

Still, I reach for her.

"Roxy," I say, pushing the thought as gently as I can into the thread of the mind-link. *"Roxy, it's me. Can you hear me?"*

For a long moment, I hear nothing. Then, the faintest, *"Leo?"*

My chest tightens. *"I'm here."*

"I thought I was dreaming," she says. Her voice in my head is quiet, frayed at the edges. *"I'm so tired. I can't shift. My arms won't stop shaking. They gave me more wolfsbane."*

"You'll be okay. They won't give you any more. I'm here now. You're not alone," I tell her. *"I'm outside watching them from the shadows. They don't know I'm here. Wait a little longer. At first light, our warriors will be here— Moon River, Golden Elm, and Ebonlight, together. You're safe. I'm here."*

They've locked her away again. But this time, she's not alone. I'll wait. I'll watch. But if they lay a hand on her—I won't stop until she's free.

THE WITCHES IN THE CIRCLE

I sit curled on the cold stone floor, my knees tucked to my chest, staring at the narrow sliver of moonlight stretching across the tower. It feels different now. Like the Moon Goddess is watching. Like She knows I'm not alone anymore.

I hear Leo through the mind-link again. *"Are you okay? What happened after they took you?"* he asks.

I draw in a shaky breath. The wolfsbane has mostly worn off now, but I still feel weak, as if my limbs belong to someone else. I'm thankful the fog in my head is gone, and I can speak to Leo. *"They brought me back here, to the tower. At first, they gave me back control of my body so I'd have the strength for what they did next, but then they held me down again. They forced more wolfsbane down my throat. I couldn't fight them."*

I have to take another deep breath to calm myself before I continue. *"After that, everything blurred. I drifted in and out, but I remember them—sitting behind me in a circle, like some twisted ritual. One by one, they took turns brushing and braiding my hair. Humming. Smiling.*

Like it was some kind of game. And every time one of them finished, she'd rise and step toward the mirror. And every time... she looked younger."

Leo doesn't respond right away. I imagine he's trying to process what I've just said. My stomach knots tighter as I continue. *"It's me. I'm keeping them young, Leo. That's what this has always been about."*

"You're not just a prisoner. You're a resource to them." His voice is soothing.

"Yes," I whisper. *"And they tricked me into believing that one of them was my mother."*

A pause, then: *"You were just a baby, Roxy. You couldn't have known."*

"I didn't understand it at first. I asked them—if only Cleonna was the one who raised me, how are the rest of them feeding off me?"

"Cleonna?"

"That's her name. The one I called Mother. But she's not the only one." I shudder, the memory slamming into me with fresh weight. *"They smiled when I asked. And then... they showed me. They all look different now, but one by one, they shifted their faces. Their voices. Their bodies. They didn't just glamorize themselves. They became her. Cleonna. Every detail— her hands, her scent, her little smile. It was like watching thirteen mirrors turn to the same reflection, and just like that, the illusion broke, and they became themselves again."*

"They all pretended to be her?" Obviously, he can't believe it either.

"They took turns being my mother, Leo. For twenty years, I thought one woman was raising me. But it was all of them. All thirteen of them take turns. One face, thirteen monsters behind it. I don't even know who I cried to. Who taught me to read, write, bake...."

A long silence stretches between us. He's still there, but he doesn't speak.

"They said I was more obedient when I believed someone cared about me."

"You were just a child." I can hear sadness in his voice.

"I know." I stand slowly and cross the room to the window. From this height, I can't see much, just the shapes of trees, the faintest glow of firelight from the clearing below. But I know he's out there. I feel him like a tether pulling me back from the edge.

"I'm sorry, Roxy."

"It wasn't your fault."

"No. But I'll make sure it ends."

I press my hand to the glass. *They can't keep pretending forever. The magic's fading. I saw their genuine faces tonight. Old. Hollow. Crumbling.*

"You'll never see them again after tomorrow. I promise."

And for the first time in hours, I believe that might be true. The sky is softening—just barely. It's that fragile moment before dawn when the darkness begins to fade. I haven't slept. I can't.

I've been sitting by the narrow window, my eyes fixed on the clearing below with my heart tuned to the bond between Leo and me. I don't see him, but I feel him. He's there–a watching, unmoving guardian in the trees.

The witch's bonfire from last night burns low. Its light glows a faint orange against the fog-hung grass. Embers shift and crackle. A few of the witches lying near it stir, their silk cloaks twisted around them like spiderwebs, their wine goblets tipped over in the dirt.

Then one of them groans and sits up. "Ugh. My head," she mutters, clutching her temple.

Another stretches, long and catlike. "That's what you get for drinking the full bottle."

"I only drank half."

"Half the case."

Laughter bubbles from a third. Her hair has come loose in tangled waves, but even in her bleary state, she looks younger than she did last night. Youth lingers in the way her skin glows and in how her eyes have brightened.

I grip the edge of the windowsill, pressing my forehead to the cool stone.

"Leo?" I whisper through the link. *"They're waking up."*

"I see them." His voice is calm, but just beneath the surface, I hear the rage.

One of the witches kicks the dying fire, sending sparks into the air. "We should go back up before the sun gets too high," she says. "She's always most potent just before dawn."

"Don't forget the wolfsbane," says a second.

I stiffen.

"We can't have her reaching out. Who knows who she'd be talking to."

They all look toward the tower then. I shrink back. My heart pounds in my chest.

"Leo... they're coming."

"I know," he growls, and this time the anger is clearer, sharper. *"They want to dull the mind-link. Break it. Poison you again."*

"I can't do this anymore," I whisper. *"I thought I was going to die."*

"You're not going to die," he says. *"They won't touch you."*

I feel his fury through the mind-link like wildfire in my chest. His wolf is ready, and on edge, but I know he's waiting. Leo is holding himself back because we need the others, but the witches are moving now.

One rises, brushing ash from her skirt, conjuring a comb from the air. Another lifts a small vial. The liquid inside is thick and dark green. It's liquid wolfsbane. They laugh as they walk toward the tower, slow and methodical, like girls rising from a party the next morning.

My body goes cold. I can't fight them. Not like this. I can barely stand. I stumble back from the window with my chest heaving and press both hands to the wall. I close my eyes. *"Leo, please."*

His response is immediate. *"I won't let them near you."*

"You said we wait—"

"Only if they don't touch you." He pauses. *"If they step inside that tower, Roxy, I will end them."*

Something tight and heavy unwinds in my chest. The fear dissipates and something else takes its place—trust.

The witches laugh again. Footsteps crunch in the grass. One of them looks up at the tower. "I can't wait to see how pretty I'll be after this braid," she says.

The first light of dawn brushes against the tower window like a breath—soft and golden. I grip the edge of the window and look out across the valley.

At first, there's only mist. Still thick in places, it curls over the grass like it's reluctant to let the night go. But then the fog is drawn back like a veil.

When I see them, I gasp.

From the hills beyond the tree line, the ridge lines are moving–prowling.

I see thousands of them–wolves, warriors, horses, and chariots.

The slope of the eastern hill is covered, the line stretching out so far that it blurs at the edge of the world. Armor catches the rising sun and gleams like fire in shades of silver, gold, black, and red. I see Moon River's colors and Golden Elm's banners. The warriors move in unison, a tide of power cresting the valley rim.

They're here. They all came.

The first golden chariots wheel into view, sleek and curved, drawn by massive white stallions, their riders armed with long spears and painted shields. Horseback riders flank them, some wielding bows, others swords, their horses' manes streaming in the morning breeze.

A cry breaks in my throat. I press my hand to the window, tears stinging my eyes. *"Leo!"*

"They came for you," he replies softly.

My whole body trembles—not from fear this time, but from something else. Something fierce. Something like love and pride bound together.

Below me, the witches haven't noticed yet. No longer stalking toward me, they're still near the fire, tossing salt into the flames, arguing about which one of them gets to braid my hair next. Some of them are laughing smugly.

They have no idea what's coming.

The warriors on the hill descend with deliberation. It's an avalanche of motion. Cloaks whip behind them. War drums thunder to life, low and steady. The sound shakes through the earth and echoes into my bones.

For a moment, I can't breathe.

I thought no one would come. Not really. I thought I would die in this tower–forgotten, used, and alone.

But they're here. They're all here.

And leading them, I see the flash of dark fur darting from the trees.

Leo.

In his wolf form, he races ahead of the others, a silent shadow streaking toward the tower. Marek follows not far behind, his silver fur glinting in the new light. I recognize others, too—faces from Moon River, from the festival, many I've never seen before because they are from the other packs. Today, they are warriors united for one thing:

To end this. For me.

The witches finally turn. One of them stands, shielding her eyes against the growing light. "What's that noise?" she asks.

Another straightens, sniffing the wind. "That's not thunder."

A third's smile fades entirely. "Someone's coming."

They all look toward the ridge just as the banners unfurl.

The moment they realize what's happening is like glass shattering. They stagger back, their voices rising, spells half-formed on their lips. They're too late. Dawn has broken, and with it, retribution.

I brace both hands on the stone as the light pours in, rising higher and higher, illuminating every inch of the valley. It's a new day, a new beginning, and finally, after all the darkness, freedom will come.

The witches finally see what's coming.

One of them shrieks, stumbling back from the fire. "There are thousands of them!"

Another drops the goblet she's holding. It shatters at her feet.

"They're coming for her," one whispers. "All of them—they're here for the girl!"

"The tower isn't safe anymore!" another howls, spinning toward the trees. "Call the rogues! Call them all!"

Chaos erupts. Several of the witches scatter into the woods, their cloaks flying and their voices rising into frantic incantations. Others run in circles, arguing about what to bring, who to blame. A long, piercing cry cuts through the valley.

The woods explode with movement. They come like shadows tearing free from the trees—hundreds of rogue wolves, pale and twisted, their eyes glowing red in the growing light. They don't run like normal wolves. They lurch, stagger, charge in uneven patterns, their jaws snapping wildly, foam dripping from their mouths.

I gasp, backing away from the window. They're everywhere, pouring into the valley like a flood.

The witches gather in a knot near the fire, raising their hands with wild eyes. Their glamour flickers and fades. Youth pulls back in flashes of old, stretched skin and cracked lips. Fear is breaking their magic, and the army hasn't even reached them yet.

The witches try to flee, but they're not fast enough. Not this time. This time, we were ready.

And I swear—they'll never cage or corrupt this world again. We'll banish them, one and all.

THE WOLVES IN THE ROGUES

Leo

THE GROUND TREMBLES BENEATH US AS THE WOLVES DESCEND FROM THE hills. Golden Elm's warriors move in perfect formation, their chariots wheeling in gleaming arcs of gold and steel. Ebonlight's dark riders thunder alongside them, their black cloaks snapping like storm clouds.

But it's not just them. Ravensong and Nightshade, two packs I hadn't counted on joining us, both answered the call.

They're here. All of them. For her.

The witches sense it, and their smug laughter curdles into panic. Then they run.

"No," I growl through the mind-link. *"Do not let them scatter."*

I break from the tree line in wolf form, dirt kicking behind my paws as I surge toward the clearing. The witches are already darting between trees, trying to vanish into shadows. But there's nowhere left to hide.

"Marek—now."

"On it."

Warriors rush in from every angle—black wolves, silver, red, gold —all fanning out in a tightening spiral.

"Form a circle around the witches," I command through the mind-link. *"Make it tight with no gaps. I want all thirteen of them surrounded. They do not leave this valley. Not one of them."*

A group of Moon River wolves peel off, flanking the clearing from both sides. Golden Elm's archers guard the tree lines. Ebonlight riders leap from horseback, shifting mid-air, their teeth bared and ready.

The witches shriek—high and feral. One throws a fire burst that scorches the side of a supply wagon. Another lifts her hands, summoning wind, trying to push us back.

"Hold the line!" I shout.

Roxy's tower is situated behind them, gleaming white in the sunlight. My chest clenches. I know she's watching.

The witches huddle near the bonfire, now sputtering against the rays of dawn. The real Cleonna—the one whose face they all used to raise Roxy in that twisted lie—bares her teeth. Her eyes flash. "Call the rogues!" she howls.

A cry echoes through the trees.

And then—they come.

The rogues burst from the forest in droves, twisted wolves with eyes like hot coals. They throw themselves at our lines in chaos, lung-ing, snapping, snarling.

"Let the other warriors handle them," I tell Marek. *"Our focus is the coven."*

He growls in response, his silver fur bristling as he flanks Cleonna from the left. I move from the right.

A second circle forms behind us, tight, disciplined, and unbreak-able. We're pushing the witches inward, herding them like prey.

They lash out wildly with fire, fog, wind, and shadows.

But it's not enough. Not anymore.

We close in. The witches cluster together now with their backs to one another. All of them are wild-eyed and breathless. There's nowhere left to run.

My fury becomes something lethal, but I don't just want vengeance. I want peace.

The witches scream and rage. But the sun fully rises behind the cliffs, cutting through the valley like a blade, and our circle holds. The witches are trapped, their spells fraying at the edges, their glamour cracking like old paint.

But something else shifts in the air. Not fear. Not chaos. Stillness.

I glance past Marek, past the ring of warriors, to where the battle raged moments ago, and stop cold.

The rogues, those skinny, feral wolves, aren't attacking. They're standing still, scattered across the valley like stunned shadows.

A few of them shake their heads, blinking as if waking from a deep sleep. One falls to its knees. Another drops its snarl and whines.

Marek stiffens beside me. *"Do you see that?"*

"Yeah," I reply. *"What the hell is happening?"*

I look closer. Their fur… it's changing. One by one, the dull, matted gray of their coats fades like soot washed from stone—revealing vibrant colors beneath. Rust-red, golden-brown, and ash-white.

They're not rogues. They're from our packs!

All across the valley, the transformation spreads like wildfire. Wolves stumble, blinking as if thrown into a new world. Warriors from our side recognize them. Cries break out—not of war, but of recognition and reunion.

"Is that—" Marek's voice breaks through the link. *"Leo, that's Dario. He vanished three weeks ago."*

I look toward where Marek's gaze is fixed. And it is. It's Dario. His coat is a sunlit auburn now, and his mate has already broken ranks to reach him, colliding with him and whimpering.

More wolves shed the gray, rediscovering their true shapes and shades. All around me, the battlefield dissolves into something else entirely: confusion, awe, heartbreak, and joy. Every pack is being reunited with lost loved ones.

"They weren't rogues," I whisper. *"They were ours all along."*

"The witches..." Marek growls low. *"They cast spells on them. They stole them and turned them into weapons."*

"Not anymore."

As the witches' grip slips, their magic fractures like shattered ice, and the truth breaks free. Near the edge of the circle, three wolves step through the parting ranks. Their snarls are quiet, deliberate. Their colors are already returning—shining through the rot.

One is deep silver with streaks of obsidian in his tail.

Corwin.

The other is lean, red coated, and golden-eyed, with a white flame-mark on his chest.

Silas.

And behind them emerges a smaller wolf with pale fur soft as snow, her eyes bright with clarity—

Harla.

They join the circle. None of them are confused or broken. They know who they are now. And they remember who did this to them. Together, they move to stand beside me and Marek.

The witches scream.

Cleonna stumbles back from the circle, her face halfway between her false youth and the crone beneath. "No!" she shrieks. "No, you were mine! You were all mine!" Her voice is shrill, trembling, cracking like glass.

The wolves growl.

Corwin lunges a step forward—not to strike, just to remind her that her power is nothing now. Without Roxy's energy to fuel it, the magic that once rippled at her fingertips is gone, hollow. His eyes burn with a fury that is centuries deep.

Silas lowers his head, his teeth bared.

Harla snarls low and long, a sound that makes even the warriors stiffen.

"You see this?" I ask Marek.

"I do." His voice is fierce and steady. *"It's over."*

The circle closes tighter. The witches press together, clutching their useless trinkets, whispering spells that crumble in the air. One tries to run. A sandy hued wolf appears from nowhere and blocks her path, growling until she stumbles back.

All across the valley, wolves find each other. The battle is over. In its place is a homecoming. But here, at the center, the thirteen witches stand alone. Their stolen army has come back to itself, and now, there is nowhere left to run.

I stand at the forefront next to Marek, my chest heaving from the desperate surge of victory. The battle has long since shifted, and what once was chaos is now stillness in the dawn air. Wolves, full of their own rediscovered strength, watch with growling restraint. More warriors stand ready behind them, ready to pounce at the first sign of the witches' resurgence—but they don't move.

One witch, tall and pale, breaks from the others, her pumpkin-orange hair dripping with sweat, her pale eyes wild and burning. She steps between Cleonna and her coven, raising a long, delicate finger to point at me.

"You!" Her voice is sharp as a blade's strike. "Alpha of Moon River!" She steps forward, her chin lifted defiantly. "You think you can banish us? Rescue your sweet princess?" Her voice echoes across the clearing.

I hold my ground with my wolf form locked in tense vigilance. *What's she planning?*

"She's reciting something... pulling ancient words," Marek's thought slices through our mind-link.

The witch's mouth moves, her voice slipping higher and louder with each syllable.

"Wolf of midnight black and flame,
Bound to river, bound to name.
Moon above, now turn your face,
Let death descend and leave no trace.
Rapunzel root and blessed bloom,
Drag him down, seal his doom.
Blood to still and breath to break,
Let the river's silence wake."

The words warble through the morning light, twisting the air around us. The other witches are watching her, silent but expectant.

Then twelve more voices rise—one after another, neat and sharp. They chant together in a chorus that shakes the valley. Alone, their magic is brittle and thin, barely more than sparks. The only way it holds any power now is when they join forces, weaving their spells into a single, unified strike.

No. No, this isn't happening. The wolves bristle all around us. Marek turns his head and bares his fangs.

I'm pinned, caught by the spell's force, unable to turn, unable to respond. My fur stands on end as the magic burns through every nerve. Fear threads behind my teeth, but I refuse to retreat. The chanting grows louder, each syllable striking the air like stones dropping into glass.

"Wolf of midnight black and flame,
Bound to river, bound to name.
Moon above, now turn your face,
Let death descend and leave no trace.
Rapunzel root and blessed bloom,
Drag him down, seal his doom.
Blood to still and breath to break,
Let the river's silence wake."

One of the witches clutches her pendant, still centered on me, her eyes alight with triumph. That's when I feel it--the world loosening. I'm weightless, like I've been plucked from the earth. They must be furious with me for starting this battle and taking Roxy from them. So furious they're willing to spend the last drops of their magic to destroy me.

"Leo!" Marek's cry cuts through the spell's haze. I jerk my head toward him. He's a snow-streaked blur at my side, his jaw open.

But the spell holds.

Higher and higher I rise, with my paws unable to reach the ground. Below me, the wolves and warriors shrink, now pale specks at the edge of my vision. My lungs scream. My mind thrashes. But the chant continues, inexorable, like rolling thunder.

I surge at Marek, clawing for strength. *"Anchor me."*

He roars back: *"Hold! Resist!"*

But they have me. The force is relentless.

My heart pounds in my chest, each beat echoing in my skull. My vision tunnels: trees, sky, smoke, the tower, but I cannot reach the earth.

And then, sudden weightlessness. The chanting stills as the spell breaks me down, taking me from the forest and emptying me out.

I hang in the air like a fallen banner, my fur limp and breath gone. I close my eyes against the world shuddering beneath me. My senses dull. The world muffles. My limbs go slack. I can't fight it anymore. I hit the ground, and the world dissolves into darkness.

THE HERO IN THE GIRL

I watch in horror as the witches' magic lifts Leo into the air, his midnight-black wolf twisting in pain, suspended like a marionette on invisible strings. The witches' chant claws through the morning.

"No!" I scream, slamming both palms against the windowsill. My voice breaks, raw and useless against the sky.

Then—they drop him.

His body hits the ground with a sickening thud. He's completely still—motionless.

A scream tears from my throat. "Somebody help me!" I shout, leaning out the window, desperate. "Please! Someone! Throw me a rope!"

Below, chaos churns through the valley. Wolves sprint, warriors cry out, magic swirls like smoke. The witches scream again, louder this time.

"Please!" I yell again. "He's—Leo's—" My voice shatters on his name.

Then, finally, someone hears me. A warrior near the supply wagon

—his armor gleaming–looks up, and without a word, he grabs a coil of rope and throws it toward the window.

On the third try, I catch it in my trembling hands but nearly drop it.

"I've got you," he calls. "Hold tight!"

I wind the rope around my bedpost and pull it taught to make sure it will hold. I brace my feet against the stone. Slowly, shakily, I begin to climb down. My arms burn, and my legs shake, but I make it.

When I finally hit the ground, the soldier's there—his brawny arms steadying me.

"Thank you," I say, my voice vibrating.

He nods once. His jaw is tight with focus. "Anything for you, Princess Roxanna." Then he turns, guiding me through the crowd to Leo, who is still lying on the ground, lifeless.

I fall to my knees. "Leo," I whisper, reaching for him. "Please. Come back."

He doesn't move.

Tears blur the world around me, but I refuse to look away. I press my palm to his back. His body is still warm, but fading fast.

The witches shriek louder.

I look up, fury and grief blooming inside me like a second heartbeat. "You won't take him." My voice shakes. "You won't take *anything* else from me ever again!" And this time, I don't feel powerless. I feel *ready*.

My hands tremble as I brush his fur. His body is far too still beneath my fingers. Leo's chest doesn't rise. His heart—no. I won't say it. I won't believe it.

My tears drip onto his dark coat. "Leo..." Barely a whisper, my voice breaks like my heart. "Please, I love you."

Around us, the circle tightens. Warriors in their wolf forms bare their teeth, holding the witches in place. None of them speak—not even the witches now. They just watch with their eyes filled with curiosity and fear.

I pull the silver band from my braid and let my hair fall wild and loose around my shoulders. It shines in the sunlight. I lean forward and let the ends of my hair cover his body, over his heart, over his silent lungs.

"Please," I beg silently. "If there's anything left in me, if there's anything the witches *couldn't* take, let it be this. Let me bring him back."

The breeze moves gently at first, brushing through the valley. My hair lifts around us, swirling like mist. Threads of golden light glimmer through the strands, then deepen—scarlet, gold, bronze, copper—magic woven into every lock.

A flicker stirs beneath my fingers. I freeze.

His ear twitches. I close my eyes and press my forehead to his.

"Come back," I whisper. "You promised me a beginning. Don't leave me now."

And then—beneath my hand—I feel it.

Thump.

My eyes fly open. His chest moves. His ribs lift with another breath.

"Leo?" My voice cracks.

His paws twitch, his ears flicker, and then his eyes open, slowly and drowsily. He's alive.

I let out a sob that's part laughter, part scream.

He blinks up at me, dazed. *"Roxy...?"*

I throw my arms around his neck, burying my face in his fur. "You're okay. Thank the Goddess, you're okay."

He groans softly, moving to press his head into my shoulder.

"I thought I lost you." I pull back, cupping his face with both hands, tears still streaking down my cheeks. "Don't you *ever* die on me again."

Behind us, the wolves howl—not in mourning, but in triumph. The witches are still trapped in the circle. Thirteen faces pale with shock.

The girl they caged has just undone death itself. She's *not* theirs anymore.

I step forward, my voice steady and loud enough to carry. "You stole me."

The witches flinch at the words, as if truth itself burns hotter than fire.

"You took me from my family—ripped me from my mother's arms while I was still a baby and locked me in a tower to be your potion, your prisoner. You lied to me every single day of my life. You used my love like a leash. You fed me stories and poison and made me believe I was safe when I was just… fuel."

I pause, the words cracking loose something deep inside me. The wolves behind me don't make a sound; they're listening. The entire valley is.

"You did that to *me*. And you did it to *them*," I continue, pointing to the wolves who now stand tall in power and strength—the ones they called rogues, the ones they nearly destroyed. "You cursed them and stole their identities. You hurt their families. You made them your weapons."

I take one step closer. The witches shrink back.

"That ends today."

Cleonna opens her mouth, maybe to argue, maybe to plead—but I lift my hand, and she goes silent again.

"I banish you from these lands. Every one of you. And hear me now—if any of us ever see your faces again, anywhere between the vineyards near Ravens Square, the banks of Moon River and Golden Elm, or the cliffs of Nightshade. If we ever catch word or wind of you near Ebonlight Pack's borders with Vaeloria or Hexeton, or in the Moonbeam Valley, you won't just be banished."

I narrow my eyes.

"You'll be *hunted*. You'll be *ended*."

Howls erupt behind me—powerful, layered, deafening. Moon River, Golden Elm, Ebonlight Ravensong, and Nightshade–five packs unified in a cry of defiance and promise.

Leo stands beside me, his voice strong through the mind-link. *"They'll never hurt any of us again. You've made sure of it."*

The witches tremble. Cleonna falls to her knees, the last shreds of her false beauty withering in the sunlight. "If you promise not to destroy us," she rasps, "we'll go."

"You'll walk," I say coldly. "On foot, all the way to the edge of the territory and beyond."

They nod, one by one, stripped of every ounce of power they once claimed.

The wolves flank the witches in silence, forming two solid lines. Under watchful eyes, the coven hobbles forward, their steps slow, broken, and full of humiliation. The wolves follow, their shoulders squared, ready to strike at the first sign of treachery.

I watch them go. The wind catches my hair, the weight of everything I've lost reclaimed and settling into my bones.

It's over. The witches are done, and the wind that rushes through the valley now feels like a breath of fresh air—clean and bright, brushing over my skin. This is the beginning of something new.

A warrior from Moon River steps forward, a bundle of clothes folded neatly in his arms. "For your Alpha and his Beta," he says with a respectful nod, his eyes gleaming.

Leo and Marek disappear behind a wagon and shift back to human form. When Leo steps out, dressed in black with Moon River's sigil on his chest, the world seems to still. He walks straight to me without hesitation, his hair tousled from shifting, his deep chestnut eyes locked on mine.

And then he kisses me.

The valley erupts in cheers. Wolves howl. Those in their human forms clap and shout, their voices echoing off the hills. It feels like sunlight breaking through years of shadow. Like hope has bloomed right here in the grass beneath our feet.

I barely have time to catch my breath when a hush falls over the crowd.

A royal couple steps forward, both regal and radiant in matching gold and crimson. A Golden Elm tree, representing their pack, adorns their cloaks. The man is tall, broad-shouldered, and his eyes are the same shade of blue as mine. The woman walks beside him, graceful as wind through leaves, her gaze locked on me.

"Roxanna," the man says softly. His voice is thick with emotion. "I am Jacob, Alpha of Golden Elm. And this... this is my mate, Lorna."

The woman's eyes brim with tears. Her hand shakes as she reaches out. "I am your mother."

The world tilts around me.

"I remember you," I whisper. My heart lurches as I stumble toward her. "I remember your voice."

She pulls me into her arms, warm and comforting, and then—softly, almost like breath—she sings.

"Sleep, my light, my shining star,

No matter how far away you are…"

The melody pierces something deep inside me. I know this. I *know* it.

"Threads of sunlight in your hair,

Weave a magic pure and rare…"

Tears spill from my eyes as I press my face into her shoulder. My lips move before I realize it.

"Fairies will guard your sleep

And gather moonbeams in the deep…"

She gasps as I join her, and then we're both crying, holding each other like the lost years might disappear if we hold tightly enough. My father's arms wrap around both of us.

"Though the night is deep and wide,

Love will always be your guide…."

My real mother. My real family.

And somehow—finally—I've come home.

THE FAMILY IN THE CASTLE

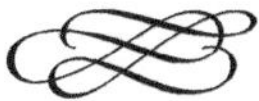

THE WITCHES ARE GONE. THE LAST RUSTLE OF THEIR TATTERED CLOAKS disappears beyond the eastern ridge, ushered by two lines of wolves who don't blink as they pass. Moonbeam Valley holds its breath as a profound silence settles over them—not one of fear or tension, but something sacred: peace.

I stand next to a dark bay stallion, offered to me by one of our warriors. The midday sun filters through the trees in golden shafts, lighting up the mist like fire. Roxy is near the edge of the clearing, talking softly with her parents, her *actual* parents, who look at her like they've been holding their breath for twenty-one years and have finally exhaled.

I let them have their moment.

Marek comes to stand beside me, already halfway through organizing our warriors. He smells of sweat and victory. His energy is focused on getting our pack home safely.

"Have you made a plan, Alpha?" he asks.

"I'm riding with Roxy to Golden Elm. I'll give her time to settle and get to know her people."

Marek follows my gaze then nods.

I take a breath and clap a hand to his shoulder. "You're in charge of getting Moon River pack home safe and whole."

Marek gives me a faint grin. "Consider it done."

I nod once. "You'll be home by dusk if you take the northern ridge."

"I'll handle it," he says. Then he leans in slightly, his voice low. "But when you get back, I expect a feast."

My lips twitch into a grin. "You'll be the first to get a plate."

He laughs and strides off, already barking orders through the mind-link. I take one more proud look at my warriors, especially the ones who have rejoined us from being under the coven's spell, then turn toward Golden Elm's pack, waiting at the edge of the clearing.

Roxy stands beside a sleek painted mare with white socks and a silver-streaked mane. Her father, Jacob, Alpha of Golden Elm, helps adjust her stirrup while her mother stands nearby with misty eyes, tucking a lock of hair behind Roxy's ear like she's done it a thousand times. I'm thankful for the horses since Roxy and I are still recovering from being attacked by the witches.

When Roxy sees me, she breaks into a small smile, soft and private. It's the kind of smile that makes the weight in my chest ease just enough to breathe again.

"You ready?" I ask, approaching her.

She nods. "I think so. I don't want to leave them yet, but... I want to go with you."

I reach up and squeeze her hand. "You're not leaving anyone. It would be my pleasure to escort you home to Golden Elm."

She blinks, and I can tell those words settle deep. "Thank you, Leo," she says earnestly.

"You just saved my life. It is the very least I can do, and if there's anything else you need or wish for, please know that you have but to ask."

We mount together, our horses stepping lightly over the churned earth of the valley. The trail toward Golden Elm winds through open fields and pine-covered hills.

Roxy rides beside me, her posture tall, but her eyes still scanning the horizon—the way wolves do when they're learning a new territory. Her fingers tighten slightly on the reins.

"What are you thinking?" I ask.

She looks over at me. "That I don't know what kind of daughter I'm supposed to be–or what kind of princess. I mean, I've only ever read about princesses in storybooks."

"You'll figure it out," I say. "The same way you figured out how to face down thirteen witches with your bare hands."

She huffs a soft laugh and rolls her eyes. "It's just so strange. All this time, I thought I had no one. And now… suddenly I have an entire pack. A family."

I watch her for a moment. "You have two packs now, Roxy. You'll never be alone again. I promise."

She swallows, blinking fast, like she's fighting back tears. We ride in silence after that, the sound of creaking leather and hoofbeats filling the space between us. For the first time since the war drums sounded, I allow myself to think beyond this moment to the pack we'll build and the alliances we've made today.

After several hours of riding, the gates of Golden Elm rise ahead, tall and carved from the heartwood of the ancient forest. Sunlight catches the golden leaves etched into the archway, and I can feel the strength of this place in my bones. This is no ordinary stronghold. This is a kingdom that stands united.

Roxy rides beside me, her eyes filled with awe and a thread of something that looks like relief and belonging. She's home in a way she never imagined possible.

When we enter the inner courtyard, warriors line the path, some with bows across their backs, others in scarlet cloaks stitched with golden thread. They bow their heads to their Alpha and Luna out of recognition and respect.

And on this day, for the first time, they gather to welcome their princess, bowing to her with reverence.

Roxy's parents dismount first, and we follow their lead. Her mother, Lorna, reaches for Roxy first, holding her close again like she's afraid letting go will wake her from a dream.

Jacob nods to me. "Walk with me, Alpha."

I dismount and follow, pausing only to brush my fingers against Roxy's shoulder in reassurance. She smiles faintly and follows her mother inside.

Jacob and I move through a side passage that opens onto a wide stone terrace overlooking the courtyard and valley below. The view is breathtaking—rolling hills, scattered meadows, and the curve of the river that winds between Golden Elm and the far borders of Nightshade.

Jacob folds his arms, standing tall in his golden cloak. His voice is steady, but his eyes never leave the horizon. "I owe you more than I can ever repay."

"You owe me nothing," I say. "She's your daughter. And I'm just glad she found her way back."

He nods slowly and then glances at me. "But you brought her home. You protected her, and you'll stand beside her. You are an honorable and noble Alpha."

"I will protect her at all costs," I say simply.

After a moment, Jacob exhales and looks toward the sunset. "We've been isolated too long. We let ourselves become separate— Golden Elm, Moon River, Nightshade, Ebonlight, Ravensong. We forgot we were meant to stand together, to be allies and fortresses in the midst of Vaeloria and Hexeton."

I nod. "The isolation ends now. We need unity more than ever. The coven must stay off our lands."

He turns fully toward me. "We need a vow. Not just for ceremony, but for the future. For the generations that follow. The witches are gone, but they won't be the last danger. Our children, your children, need more than a memory to keep them safe. They will need this alliance."

"They'll have it," I say. "Moon River will stand with Golden Elm—

in formal recognition, shared watch posts along the border trails, joint patrols during full moons, solstices, and equinoxes."

"Ebonlight will follow," Jacob says. "They've always been fierce, but they know loyalty. And Ravensong—"

"The Luna of Ravensong sent her warriors because they believed in what we were fighting for," I explain. "She's an outstanding leader. They'll stay if we give them a good reason to."

We shake hands then—not as strangers or even just allies, but as two Alphas with hearts for their packs.

Behind us, a door creaks softly. Lorna steps onto the terrace. Her eyes meet mine and soften. "Thank you for bringing her back to us."

I swallow hard. "I'm sorry I didn't find her sooner."

"But you did find her," she says. "And she found herself." She walks to Jacob's side, looping her arm through his.

"We have a long road ahead," Jacob says. "We'll need to mend the old paths and help her become acquainted with her new life."

"We'll do it," I promise. "Together."

The doors swing open behind us, and Roxy appears in the archway, her eyes brimming with joy.

"You have to see the library," she says, beaming. "It has three levels filled with thousands of books, and there's a spiral staircase in the middle with sliding ladders on every floor."

Roxy steps into my arms without hesitation. I wrap her up, holding her close as she talks, her excitement bubbling over.

"And there's a balcony off the west wing with an old brass telescope mounted to the rail. You can see clear to the tree line. The castle, Leo, is like something out of a dream. Everyone's so kind, and the kitchen staff baked cookies just for me."

Jacob chuckles. "They were ready to crown her twice over. Word's spread. You two didn't just banish a coven. You brought home pack members we thought we'd lost forever."

"It's true," Lorna adds. "Some of those wolves wandered the forests for years, believed dead, and now—" Her voice catches. "Now they're home. They're *alive*. And my baby girl is alive. All thanks to the two of you."

"It wasn't me," I say. "Roxy banished the coven and saved me, too."

Roxy lowers her chin, trying in vain to hide a blush.

The courtyard below us is starting to fill with color—crimson and gold banners waving in the wind, people moving toward the center square. A drum beats faintly from below.

"What's going on down there?" I ask.

"A celebration," Jacob replies with a smile. "We didn't exactly plan it, but the people need it."

By the time we descend the terrace steps, the square is alive with music. Shifters in human form greet long-lost siblings, parents, and mates. Tables overflow with food and pitchers of cider. Children chase each other, their laughter echoing off the stone castle walls.

Voices ring out from every direction—old friends reunited, families dancing in circles. This is a celebration that belongs to them, and only them. No visiting packs. No formal alliances. Just the people of Golden Elm, with Roxy at the heart of it all.

She dances with her mother first, the two of them laughing. I watch her spin, radiant and free, her joy as untamed as it's ever been. She's not a prisoner in a tower anymore. She's their princess now.

Jacob claps me on the shoulder as he passes with a tankard of cider. "She's got her people back," he says.

I nod because he's right. This celebration—it isn't just for Roxy. It's for what was stolen from this whole pack—and what they've reclaimed.

****

Three days have passed since we banished the witches and celebrated, and Roxy and I are still at the Golden Elm castle.

The sun shines softly through an apple orchard, dappling the grass in patches of warm gold. We walk beneath rows of trees heavy with ripening fruit. Roxy's hand is laced through mine while Jacob and Lorna stroll just ahead of us.

"It's beautiful here," I say quietly.

Roxy nods. "It feels like a piece of you, Mother," she murmurs, glancing toward the Luna. "Everything you touch seems to bloom."

Lorna turns back with a grin. "I do love growing fruit and flowers."

"This orchard has been in our family for generations," Jacob adds. "It's where I proposed to your mother."

"Really?" Roxy asks, smiling.

"She said no the first time," he teases.

"I said *not yet,*" Lorna corrects him with a smirk.

We all laugh, the sound light and unburdened.

Roxy disappears to pick apples with her mother, their voices soft and cheerful. I watch them for a moment, Roxy's golden hair catching in the twilight like fire and silk, strands of strawberry shining brighter now that she's back with her own pack.

"I've walked these paths for years," Jacob says. "I planted most of this myself, but I never imagined I'd one day walk them with my daughter's mate."

There's something heavy beneath his words. Something complicated. I let the silence sit between us for a moment before answering.

"I know this can't be easy," I say.

He nods slowly. "It's not. I don't know her, not really. I know what was taken, but I can't pretend I was there. I didn't hold her when she cried. I didn't teach her to read or watch her fall asleep by the fire. I missed all of it."

I glance at him, surprised at how open he's being. "That must've been heartbreaking for all of you. You can get to know her now."

"And I am so grateful for that opportunity, but every moment I get with her feels like a borrowed gift, and I don't want to lose her again."

"Roxy's safety comes before everything. And keeping the witches far from our lands is right behind it. You'll never have to fear losing her again—not to them, not to anyone. I'd lay down my life before I let that happen." We come to a stop beneath a wide-armed oak. Its branches stretch like a canopy overhead. "Alpha, I must ask you," I say, my voice steady, though my heart threatens to beat out of my chest.

Jacob looks at me patiently.

"May I have your blessing to ask Roxy to be my Luna?"

"The truth is, Leo," he says with a proud smile, "it was never mine to decide. The Moon Goddess chose long before I ever met you. You and Roxy are meant for each other."

I nod once. "We are."

He exhales slowly. "I don't believe in standing between a bond like that, and I don't think Roxy needs anyone's permission to live the life she chooses. She's proven she can fight her way through anything."

"I agree," I say. "But I also know what it means to be her partner, and I would never take that lightly."

He studies me for a long moment. "Then I'll say this instead: I won't pretend I know her the way I should, but I love her all the same. Fiercely. I missed the first twenty-one years of her life, and I'll never get those back, but I want her in our lives. I want her to know this is home."

"You have my word," I say. "I'm not taking her away from you. She'll always have family here. I want her to have that. We'll visit often. Whenever she wants."

His jaw flexes like he's biting back more emotion than he's willing to show. Then, he claps a firm hand on my shoulder. "You have my blessing. Just don't make her choose between you and us."

"She won't have to," I say. "She's already chosen both."

Jacob gives me a small, grateful smile. "Then I think we're going to be all right." He looks past me, toward the orchard where Roxy walks with Lorna, their heads bent together, laughter ringing out between the trees.

"She's already changing this place," he murmurs. "Bringing it back to life."

I smile. "That's what she does."

Roxy doesn't have to choose between packs or families. She's finally home, and whatever the future brings, she won't face it alone.

THE CROWN ON THE PRINCESS

Roxy

Golden Elm is like something out of a dream I was never allowed to have. The castle is woven into the hillside with silver stone. There's a gentleness to it—strong, but warm–not like the cold tower I was locked in. This place feels... alive.

My mother—*Lorna*, I remind myself, trying to wrap my heart around the word—leads me through the grand archway. Her hand brushes mine gently, not pulling, just offering. I take it.

"It's not as grand as some of the others," she says with a smile, "but it's home."

Home. That word lands hard in my chest.

Inside, the halls are lined with tapestries in red and gold. Light pours through stained glass windows, and servants and guards alike bow their heads as we pass, treating me like a daughter coming home.

My mother leads me up a staircase that curves like the limb of a tree, the railing polished smooth by time and hands. We don't speak as we climb. There's too much between us: grief, wonder, hope, and years lost.

We reach a hallway with a wooden door carved with delicate flowers and stop before it.

"I came here often," she says softly. "Even when everyone said we had to move on. I couldn't. Not from you."

She pushes the door open. It's a child's bedroom.

Soft light spills across a lilac hued canopy bed. The walls are painted with mint green vines and tiny glimmering fairies. There's a little rocking chair in the corner and shelves still lined with picture books and carved toys. A faded mobile of stars and leaves hangs above the bed, gently swaying in the breeze from the open window, and the ceiling is painted with vibrant yellow sunflowers.

I step inside slowly, like the room might shatter it if I breathe too hard.

"You left it like this," I whisper.

She nods, her eyes shining. "We never gave up on you."

I walk to the bed and trail my fingers across a quilt of golds and creams, stitched with tiny moons. My throat tightens. I suddenly feel like I'm five years old. Tears blur my vision, and when I turn, she's there. Her arms are open, trembling.

I step into them.

We hold each other in the center of a room that was always waiting for me. For the first time in my life, I feel it—not just safety, not just belonging, but *love.*

"I'm home," I whisper.

She presses her lips to my temple, breathing me in. "Yes, sweetheart. You are."

When she pulls back from our embrace, her eyes still glassy with emotion, she smiles, and gently asks, "Would you like some tea?"

I nod, and she takes my hand like it's the most natural thing in the world. We walk together through the corridor, our footsteps soft on the stone, until we reach the kitchen tucked at the back of the castle.

A young servant girl curtsies when she sees us. "Tea, please," my mother says kindly, "and the fresh lemon cakes."

"They came out of the oven just minutes ago, Luna," the girl replies with a grin.

Soon, a tray is brought to us in porcelain cups painted with gold leaves, steam curling from the spout of a rose-colored teapot. A small plate piled with delicate lemon cakes sits between us, their sugared tops still warm to the touch.

We sit at a little table in the corner. My mother pours for both of us, her movements graceful and unhurried.

For a long moment, we just sip and savor. Our silence is comfortable. The lemon cakes melt on my tongue—tart, sweet, and somehow nostalgic. I didn't grow up here, and yet everything feels familiar. Like this place has been quietly waiting for me to find it again.

"Your mate has a good head for leadership, and your father says he carries himself like someone twice his age."

I look at her. "He does. Leo has rescued me more than once, and in many different ways."

She glances over, a smile curving her mouth. "You are blessed by the Moon Goddess, Princess Roxanna."

Princess.

The word makes me freeze—not because it's unwelcome but because it's unfamiliar… and for the first time, it feels real.

I look around again at the castle. This is mine. I was born to it, and it's waited for me all this time.

"I never had a coronation," I murmur.

"No," she says gently. "You didn't." Then she takes my hand. "I would love to plan one with you," she says, her voice bright with excitement. "Not just as a formality—but as a celebration. Of your return. Of your strength."

I blink at her, heart swelling. "You mean it?"

She nods. "You deserve to stand before our people, not just as a survivor, but as their Princess."

A laugh bubbles out of me—light, shocked and a little shaky. "What would it even look like?"

"Oh, we'll make it beautiful," she says, her eyes alight. "We'll hold it in the Great Hall, the same one where Jacob and I were crowned. And the ball will be held in the Celestial Hall. You'll wear a crown of Golden Elm leaves and moonstone, just like mine."

My throat tightens. I didn't know how much I wanted this until I heard her say it. Not just a dress and a crown, but this place, its history, and these people.

"I'd love that," I whisper.

She squeezes my hand. "Then let's start planning."

The next few days pass in a golden blur of planning and promise.

Every morning begins in the breakfast nook with my mother. She brings a basket of fresh bread and berry preserves, and we sit with parchment spread between us—sketches, lists, ideas written in looping royal purple ink. The coronation will be held at sunset in the Great Hall. It will be grand and joyful.

"The people need something hopeful to believe in," she tells me as she sketches the outline of a floral arch. "They need to see that the darkness didn't win."

We meet with tailors who bring bolts of silk in soft golds, moonlight silver, and bright reds. Florists visit the gardens and point out which blooms will be in full flower for the ceremony. We choose music, dancers, and a menu.

Leo leaves on the fourth morning, riding toward Moon River to gather his pack and deliver the invitations to my coronation himself. I stand on the balcony and watch him go, the dark curve of his back straight and strong against the horizon.

"I'll be back soon," he'd promised, pressing his forehead to mine. "And I'll bring people who love you back with me."

I already miss him, but the time apart has its own kind of sweetness. It gives me space to get to know my family and new friends, especially those who work in the castle, which buzzes with preparations.

Ribbons string through every corridor, golden leaves pressed into the candle sconces. The kitchen staff begin preparing the first rounds of sweets and spiced wines. Even the townspeople join in. I see them painting signs, weaving flowers, and hanging lanterns across the market square.

Everywhere I go, I hear my name.

"Princess Roxy," someone calls shyly as I pass through the gardens, "welcome home."

For the first time in my life, it feels true—I belong here. Not as a secret, not as a prisoner, but simply as myself. As Roxy, the daughter of this land. The one who helped set it free.

A ball will follow the coronation—a night of celebration not only for me, but for every pack, every kingdom that stood against the witches. From Golden Elm to Nightshade, Ebonlight to Ravensong, to the riverbanks of Moon River, they'll all gather here under one sky, not just for ceremony, but to rejoice in unity.

A new chapter is beginning for me, and this time, I'll be the one writing it.

***

The castle hums with life from the moment the sun rises on the day of my coronation. Music drifts through the corridors, soft and bright. Laughter echoes from the courtyard below.

I'm in my bedroom, sitting near the window, when there's a soft knock.

"Come in," I call.

My mother enters, her smile radiant. She carries a basket full of wildflowers fresh from the meadow.

"It's time," she says gently.

She brushes out my hair with quiet care, her fingers smoothing through each lock like she's memorizing the feel of me. Then she begins to braid down the center, weaving in tiny blossoms.

"I used to imagine doing this," she whispers. "I dreamed of what you'd look like at this age, what kind of girl you'd be."

I blink back sudden tears. "I'm still figuring that out."

She kisses my temple. "You're everything I hoped for."

She helps me into a gown the color of late summer honey, embroidered with tiny crimson leaves and vines that shimmer when I move. I slip on the delicate circlet they had made just for today—Golden Elm leaves wrought into a crown, each one made of a different shade of moonstone.

The Great Hall is full when we arrive. Guests from all five allied packs stand shoulder to shoulder. Banners display Moon River's silvery blue, Ebonlight's black and crimson, Nightshade's deep violet, Ravensong's rich navy, and of course, Golden Elm's red and gold.

I spot Leo instantly. He's near the front, standing tall beside Marek and Hanna. His eyes find mine and soften with pride.

Trumpets sound, and drums beat—a low, steady rhythm that echoes in my chest. We step onto the raised platform built beneath the archway of braided vines and flowers. My father, Alpha Jacob Duskborne, lifts his voice.

"Today, we gather in triumph. The witches are gone, our lands are safe, and the girl we lost has returned—not as a victim, but as our greatest victory!"

Cheers erupt, but he raises his hands and continues.

"It is my honor to present to you the rightful heir of Golden Elm. The one who stood against darkness, who freed the lost, who carries both strength and compassion in equal measure—Princess Roxanna."

The crowd cheers louder, the sound crashing over me like a wave. Howls and applause, drums, trumpets, and voices echo through the room. My mother steps forward and places the circlet gently on my head.

"Welcome home, my daughter," she says.

I lift my chin, my heart pounding, and look out over the sea of faces. Leo smiles, fierce and full of love, and for the first time, I feel it deep in my bones. This is who I was meant to be.

After the ceremony, everyone gathers in the ballroom known as the Celestial Hall. Lanterns are strung from the rafters, their soft light glittering like stars. Musicians play in the corner, spinning a lively reel that gets feet tapping and people laughing. The scent of honey oat cakes and wild blueberries wafts through the air, mingling with peach cobbler and fresh cream. It feels like joy has been bottled and spilled across every inch of this room.

I spin in a circle, my gown fanning out in waves of gold and scarlet silk, and I can't help smiling. I've never felt more like myself. Like everything I'd been reaching for is suddenly within my grasp.

Leo catches me by the waist, pulling me into a dance. His eyes are warm and shining, and his black suit is sharp against the lantern light. "You're glowing," he says.

"I'm happy," I reply, grinning up at him. "And maybe a little dizzy."

He twirls me once more and laughs, pulling me into his arms. "Then, I'll hold you steady."

Nearby, Marek lifts a drink with Hanna at his side. The two of them argue about which dance step is actually traditional and which one he just made up. Hanna rolls her eyes and nudges him toward the floor. "Come on. Show me, then."

Even Corwin and his mate are here, both looking happy and at peace. Silas chats with Harla and Briar near the dessert table, all three of them laughing like they were never apart. The black magic is truly gone now. I can see it in the ease of their bodies, the light in their eyes. They're free.

Moon River and Golden Elm wolves mingle, trading stories, sipping wine, stealing kisses beneath the garlands. It doesn't feel like many separate packs anymore. It feels like one family.

My father appears beside me, offering his arm with surprising grace. "May I have this dance, Princess?"

I blink, touched. "Are you a good dancer?" I tease.

"Hardly," he admits with a grin. "But I'll fake it."

We dance together, and though he stumbles once, we laugh and keep going. His grip is steady, familiar in a way I never thought I'd get to know.

"You've made this place more joyful just by being here," he murmurs.

"I'm just trying to catch up on everything I missed."

"You're not just catching up, Roxy. You're creating something new—something that was never there before."

As the song ends, he spins me back toward Leo, who doesn't even ask, but just sweeps me into another dance.

When the band shifts to a slower, sweeter tune, the room hushes. People pair off and couples move closer. My mother dances with my father beneath the archway of vines, while Marek steals Hanna away for a spin that makes her swoon.

I rest my head against Leo's chest, listening to his heartbeat, and we slow dance together.

When the song ends, Leo takes my hand and leads me out of the ballroom, slipping us through the grand doors and into the cool night. We walk in silence down the lantern-lit path, past the hedges and rose-draped trellises, until the music fades behind us.

The moon hangs high over the garden, silver light spilling across the grass. Laughter and music drift faintly through the trees, softened by distance. I step beyond the reach of the last lantern, and a chill catches me. I shiver, and Leo slips his cloak around my shoulders.

Then, he reaches into the inner pocket of his shirt and pulls out a small velvet pouch. "This was my mother's," he says softly. "She wore it on her wedding day."

I hold my breath as he unties the pouch and draws out a necklace —silver braided like the river's current, light but strong. The pendant is a crescent moon carved from diamond. Curled inside the moon's curve is a tiny black wolf, etched perfectly, its head lifted in a silent howl. Just beneath it hangs a sapphire teardrop. The clasp is shaped like two crossing wolf fangs, sharp and fierce, a quiet promise of protection.

I swallow hard as he fastens it around my neck, his fingers brushing my skin. I press the pendant against my chest. "It's stunning, Leo."

"I already gave you a ring," he says, almost sheepishly. "But I still want to ask."

I turn toward him, my heart racing.

"I know you're still getting to know your family. I know you need time to find your place here," he says. "But wherever you go, I'll go. Wherever I am, there's a place for you, always."

I blink back tears. "Leo…"

"Will you be my Luna?" he asks.

I nod before the words even come. "Yes. Of course, yes."

He exhales, something in him relaxing completely, and he leans in.

When our lips meet, he wraps his arms around me, holding me steady.

In the hush of the garden, with stars above and home in every direction, I say, "Yes," again.

THE HORSES IN THE WOODS

Leo

Three weeks later…

The moon is waning gibbous–three days until it's full. Three days until I marry Roxy.

My paws press into the moss, every muscle taut and ready. Today is Roxy's first hunt. It's an important rite, a moment she's been preparing for. Marek, Hanna, Harla, Corwin, and I flank her, moving like shadows through the trees, silent and sharp.

Roxy's wolf is smaller, immature, but her eyes burn with fierce determination. She's nervous. I can feel it through our bond. But she's also proud. This is her moment to prove herself not just as our Luna, but as a warrior of Moon River.

Ahead, the elk graze in a clearing, calm and unsuspecting. The moonlight filters through the canopy, dappling their tawny backs with light. The herd is large enough to feed us all and celebrate the wedding with honor. Roxy's shoulders tense as she catches the scent on the wind, her tail flicking in quiet focus.

"Remember your training," I whisper through the mind-link. *"Stay with the pack. Move with us."*

We fan out, surrounding the clearing like a net tightening. Marek moves to the left, silent and steady. Hanna and Harla flank right. Corwin is just behind me, his eyes locked on the biggest bull elk: the prize. My pulse quickens as we draw nearer, the thrill of the hunt pulsing through every nerve.

The chase begins. Roxy's wolf bursts forward, her legs pumping, her heart racing with wild joy. I sprint beside her, proud and steady, my breath even and controlled. The elk scatter, startled, their hooves thudding against the soft earth. The bull charges with his antlers raised. He's a magnificent beast—enormous and fierce.

Hanna moves in, swift and precise, cutting off the elk's path. Marek and Corwin close the circle, forcing the herd back toward us. Roxy leaps, agile and fast, weaving through the chaos. Her eyes are bright with the hunt's fire.

I see my chance and take it. Pushing forward, I focus on the bull. My muscles coil like springs. With a surge, I knock the beast off balance, sinking my teeth into the thick hide just behind its shoulder. The bull bellows in shock and pain, thrashing wildly, but the pack is relentless.

Roxy comes in beside me, her teeth flashing, determination burning through her every move. Together, we bring the elk down.

Panting, my adrenaline still roaring, I glance at Roxy's eyes, fierce, wild, and alive. She's done it. Not just the hunt but more. She's stepped fully into her place with us, as a wolf, a warrior, a mate.

Not far off, I hear the pounding of hooves and the low grunt of a falling elk. I lift my head just in time to see Harla and Corwin emerge from the trees, their pelts streaked with blood and mud, dragging a large bull elk. Harla lets out a sharp, triumphant howl, and Corwin bumps his shoulder into hers with a low growl of approval. They fought like one body—quick, coordinated, and ruthless. It's good to see them like this, alive and whole again.

A heartbeat later, Marek and Hanna burst from the underbrush on the far ridge, chasing a smaller buck through the clearing. Marek darts left while Hanna angles from the right. In perfect sync, they leap. Marek's jaws clamp down on the neck, and Hanna slams into the hindquarters. The elk crumples beneath them.

They stand panting over the kill, Hanna's tail wagging slightly before she tosses her head back and howls. Marek joins in, deep and steady.

We've all claimed something today. Not just meat for the feast—but proof. Proof that we're strong, still wild, still a pack. That we can hunt and laugh and celebrate again. That we're whole.

The pack gathers around the fallen elk, quiet reverence settling over us. Through the mind-link, Marek hums a low chant of thanks to the Moon Goddess, and Hanna offers a prayer for the spirit of the elk.

I nuzzle Roxy gently, pride swelling in my chest. *"You were incredible."*

She howls. *"We did it. Together."*

Under the cover of ancient trees, surrounded by the pack, I know this hunt isn't just about food. It's about trust, strength, and the unbreakable bonds that hold us and our future together.

After the hunt, we move swiftly until we reach the clearing where we left our satchels hidden beneath the low boughs. The pack settles quietly as we shift back into human form—our muscles stretching and fur receding. Roxy pulls out clothes, and I follow suit, slipping into rough-spun trousers and a worn wool shirt. The others do the same, dressing quickly, the pine trees and darkness our privacy.

With the elk loaded into the mule wagon, we get ready to haul the heavy carcasses back to the village.

As we tread deeper into the heart of the woods—Harla and Hanna driving the wagon, the rest of us in the back with our prizes—the moon is the only source of light through the shroud of trees. Then, ahead—we see a shimmer, a glow as well as movement that doesn't belong.

I use the mind-link to tell Hanna to halt the wagon. There, beyond the thicket, are the evil witches' enchanted flying horses.

They hover among the ancient pines, their wings folded close, their coats shimmering with an unearthly light. Each horse glows faintly—silver-blue, rose-gold, smoky gray, and deep obsidian—like pieces of the night sky given animal form. Their eyes gleam with magic, and my heart races with caution.

These aren't ordinary horses. They are creatures of darkness, bred and bound to witches. I expect them to be fierce and dangerous. I glance at Roxy. Her gaze is steady but curious. "Stay close," I murmur.

Corwin leans toward me, his voice low. "They're watching us, but they aren't moving to attack."

We wait, our muscles coiled, our breath steady. The horses shift their weight. Soft whinnies vibrate through the air. One of them steps forward. She's a tall mare glowing in hues of blue and lavender, her wings spreading wide in slow, majestic arcs.

Her eyes meet mine, unblinking. I feel a pulse of something wild but not cruel. I carefully climb from the wagon and approach. Slowly, I lower my head in a cautious greeting.

Roxy is right behind me. The mare snorts softly, her nostrils flaring, and lowers her head toward Roxy's outstretched hand. I feel the air around us vibrating with magic—not dark, but curious, almost hopeful.

Harla murmurs, "Maybe they've been waiting for freedom, or for someone to trust."

I take a step closer. My heart is pounding. The mare nudges Roxy gently then turns and trots a short distance, pausing to look back. It's an invitation.

We're a pack and family, bound by trust and survival, and if these horses are willing to follow, maybe it's a chance to reclaim something that was once dark.

I signal for Roxy and the others to move forward. The horses stir, their wings unfurling with soft rustles like the breeze through leaves. One by one, they lift into the air, hovering a few feet above the ground.

They don't fly away. Instead, they move slowly, circling us in a protective arc before settling into a steady, gentle pace.

The lavender-blue mare steps close, letting her nose brush Roxy's shoulder. I catch the wonder in Roxy's eyes.

We follow the horses as they glide above the forest floor, lifting and floating just enough to clear low branches and brush. The moonlight dances across their coats, casting shimmering patterns on the earth below them.

The journey back to Moon River is electric. No one breaks the quiet. The forest seems to hold its breath as we move together, wolf shifters and enchanted horses, bound by a new kind of hope.

As we approach the edge of Moon River village, the horses slow, landing gracefully on the ground. They stay close, as if sensing the safety of our home. We gather around, their eyes reflecting the same mixture of awe and cautious trust I feel.

Roxy runs a hand along the mare's neck, whispering soft words. The horses are no longer symbols of fear but of possibility, proof that even things born in darkness can choose the light.

Tonight, the forest has given us a gift: new allies, new strength. The enchanted horses, still shimmering faintly with moonlit magic, are ushered into the meadow just beyond the village's edge. They step lightly, their wings fluttering, tails flicking as they explore their new freedom, their eyes bright and friendly.

With the horses safely settled, the others disperse. Hanna and Roxy head inside our house to discuss wedding plans. Corwin and Harla drive the mule-led wagon straight to the butchers and cooks waiting for the elk.

That leaves Marek and me alone beside the quiet meadow. He sits next to me with his boots kicked out in front of him. He scans the dark treetops. My friend doesn't speak, just passes me a flask and lets the silence settle.

"She's changed everything," I say finally, my voice low. "I used to think I'd lead this pack alone. No mate. No Luna. Just... duty." I pause, rolling the flask between my hands. "I told myself I was fine with that. That it was enough."

"You were lying to yourself."

"Maybe," I admit with a shrug. "I had to."

The wind stirs the trees, and I think of the first time I saw her shift. That moment she ran ahead of me through the woods, her golden fur catching the moonlight like fire. Like she belonged to the stars, the river, and everything in between.

"I was a good Alpha before I met Roxy," I say. "I kept us safe and followed the old ways, but I didn't know how great we could be until she got here."

Marek nods slowly, his gaze far off. "She's got something, that girl."

"She's got everything," I say, and I mean it. "Heart. Guts. Fire. She stood in a field of enemies and brought me back from the dead. She banished a coven with nothing but truth and a spine of steel."

"She's also a menace with morning meetings," Marek mutters.

I laugh under my breath. "She keeps me on my toes."

"And makes you happier than I've ever seen you," he adds, more serious now.

I look down at the ring on my finger—the twin to hers. We've both been wearing them since she said yes. It makes everything feel more real, more grounded.

"She's made Moon River better," I say. "And she made me better, too. I didn't even know I needed someone until she showed up."

Marek leans back on the grass with his arms folded behind his head as I watch the magical horses graze in the distance. "You know," he says, glancing over at me, "if you'd told me a year ago that the most elusive place in all of Vaelorian territory would turn into the heart of joy and laughter, I'd have said you were dreaming."

I grin, stretching out beside him. "Yeah, well... Roxy doesn't just dream. She creates."

He huffs a quiet laugh. "Moonbeam Valley used to be sacred. Secret. The Moon Goddess guarded it Herself, right? And then the witches came—built that cursed tower like a wound in the land. They trapped her there and fed her lies until she didn't know what was real."

I nod. My jaw tightens. "It was a prison, cast with magic spells from base to roof in darkness. It was a pleasure to tear it down. Roxy had a vision for it. It took a few weeks, but with the help of Golden Elm pack members, we cleared the rubble, flattened the stone, and burned the dead wood. Then, we let the wildflowers grow," I say, smiling at the memory. "And Roxy brought her vision to life."

Marek chuckles. "I still can't believe there's a merry-go-round."

"She insisted on it," I say with a shrug. "Now, the valley's unrecognizable in the best way. The brook's full of pups fishing and splashing. The lake's a bustling beach, perfect for swimming. There's this ring of trees that catches the breeze just right—it's got hammocks strung all around it that are great for lazy afternoons and shaded picnics."

"And the carousel?"

"The center of it all," I say with a laugh. "It glows with lanterns at night."

He shakes his head, but he's smiling. "And the food stalls…"

"They sell berry tarts, wildflower honey, fried bread, lemonade, and cider," I say, ticking them off on my fingers. "There's a stage now too—for dances, music, speeches. And fireworks on feast days."

Marek exhales. "It's not a secret or hidden anymore."

"No," I agree. "It's neutral ground that belongs to everyone. All five packs send people there—no territory lines, no disputes. Just wolves being wolves–laughing and living."

He glances sideways at me. "She made that happen."

I nod. "She's the reason Nightshade warriors trade stories with Ravensong healers. Why pups from both sides of the mountains build forts together out of mud and branches. She took something dark and turned it into light."

"And that's where the wedding will be?"

"Yeah," I say quietly. "Three nights from now during the full moon in the center of Moonbeam Valley. There'll be music, dancing, and long tables covered with food. Wolves from every pack are invited to gather, not as strangers, but as kin."

He nods, a faint grin tugging at his mouth. "So, are you ready for marriage?"

I glance out toward the trees, imagining her on our wedding day.

"Yes. I'm ready for her to be my Luna. Speaking of, I should probably head in," I say, pushing to my feet and brushing off my pants. "I want to see what Roxy's up to. If she's found a way to add fireworks *and* fire dancers to the wedding, I need to prepare myself."

Marek smirks, standing up beside me. "Better you than me, Alpha."

I chuckle, clapping him on the shoulder. "You should check on Hanna. Last I saw her, she was sweet-talking one of these flying horses with a handful of candied ginger."

Marek laughs, "Goddess help me, she'll have one of them sleeping in our living room."

"And as Alpha, I wouldn't dream of stopping her," I call after him then turn toward home.

Our house smells like rosemary and warm bread. Roxy lights a candle in the center of the table and sets down a plate. Her hair's in a loose braid, her cheeks flushed from the hunt. She hums as she pours cider into our mugs, and I don't think I've ever seen anything more perfect than her in my life.

She sits across from me, sliding a dish of roasted vegetables to the center of the table. "Midnight snack?" she asks, grinning. "I don't think there's any dark magic left in the horses. They're not bound anymore. I can feel it."

"I agree. They would've followed the witches if they were bound to the coven. We'll give them a choice," I say. "But if they stay, I've got a plan."

Roxy arches a brow. "Oh?"

"They can scout the borders. Patrol from the skies. We've never had eyes like that before. Not even our fastest wolves can cover ground like they can."

Her smile grows. "You want to make them guardians."

I nod. "If they're willing. They'd be a gift to every allied pack."

Roxy nods. "Then, first thing in the morning, we should ask them."

"Do you know their language already?" I wink.

"Perhaps..." she says mischievously. "Also, you're not allowed to make fun of me for making another wedding list."

I smirk. "You? A list? I'm shocked."

She tosses a piece of carrot at me. "This is important! It's not just the wedding. It's the *everything* after."

I lean forward, my elbows on the table. "All right, let's hear it."

She lifts a folded sheet of parchment from her lap. "First—ceremony timing. Do we want the vows right at moonrise? Or just after?"

"Right at moonrise," I say. "Let the Moon Goddess witness every word."

She nods, scribbling. "Agreed. Second—do we want Marek to speak, or do you think he'll cry?"

"He'll cry no matter what. Let him speak."

She laughs louder now. "Okay. Third—what's our plan after the wedding? We will be giving speeches at the celebration. We need to prepare something for the packs–for the kingdoms."

I swallow a bite of food then meet her eyes. "We keep building what we started. Golden Elm, Moon River, Nightshade, Ebonlight, Ravensong—we're stronger together. We protect one another. We'll have open trade, open festivals, and a patrol rotation."

"Monthly gatherings in Moonbeam Valley?" she adds, her eyes lighting up. "And a shared council. Not just Alphas—healers, warriors, even the elders."

"Everyone gets a voice," I say, nodding. "We stop waiting for danger to unite us. We lead with peace."

Her smile stretches wide. "You know, I used to think the world was something that happened *to* me. Now I feel like I'm part of it."

"You are the *heart* of it."

She reaches across the table, lacing her fingers with mine. The candle crackles. Outside, the river hums.

We talk late into the night—about the feast menu, and whether Silas should be allowed to bring fireworks again (no), and what we'll plant in the pack's new communal garden. We sketch out ideas for a new school near the southern edge of Moon River. We imagine pups running through Moonbeam Valley without fear. The future is ours, and we'll build it together.

Moonlight streams in through the bedroom window, casting soft silver across the wooden floor. The world outside is quiet—just the hush of the river and the occasional rustle of wind through the trees. Inside, it's safe and warm.

Roxy climbs into bed beside me, her braid loose and her skin glowing in the moonlight. She sinks into the blankets with a soft sigh, rolling onto her side to face me. Her hand finds mine beneath the covers like it always does. Easy. Natural.

"You know what I'm most excited for?" she murmurs. Her voice is soft and sleepy.

"What's that?"

"Waking up next to you every morning. After we're married, after all the excitement… just that. Just us."

My chest tightens—not from worry or fear, but from something quieter. Something whole. "You already have me," I say. "The rest is just a ceremony."

She smiles. "Still, I like the ceremony part."

I chuckle and lean in, pressing a kiss to her forehead. "Me too. And Roxy… your first hunt—you were amazing out there."

She looks up at me, smiling, warmth lighting her eyes. "Thank you, Leo. I couldn't have done it without you all. It felt good to tap into my wolf and use my instincts."

Roxy moves closer, her head tucked beneath my chin, her breath warm against my collarbone. I hold her like I always do—one arm around her back, the other draped across her waist. Her heartbeat is steady beneath my palm, and mine slows to match it.

We don't talk about the past tonight. Not the tower. Not the witches. We don't need to. That part of the story is behind us. We lived it. We survived it. Now, we get to live something new.

I've fought battles, led warriors, and faced witches, death, and doubt. But lying here with her, in this quiet house, I feel like I've finally arrived.

This is what it's all for. Not power. Not revenge. Just love. Just home.

Roxy's breathing deepens. She's already drifting off, warm and safe in my arms. The last thing I feel before I fade is her fingers curled gently against my chest.

And the last thing I think is: Soon, she'll be my wife.

THE WOMAN IN THE GOWN

Roxy

THE TENT FLUTTERS SOFTLY IN THE COOL TWILIGHT AIR. INSIDE, I SIT quietly on a cushioned stool, trying to steady my racing heart.

My gown hangs from a cedar hook near the center post of the tent, swaying gently with the breeze. It's ivory and luminous, with silver vines shimmering along the bodice, embroidered by hand, and tiny moonstones stitched into the hem and train. It looks like it was made from the stars for the Moon Goddess, spun from mist and light.

I chose it days ago, but seeing it now—waiting—I feel everything all at once: wonder, love, and peace.

My mother steps closer, her eyes glistening. "You're the daughter I always dreamed of. This day is for you, Roxanna."

I swallow hard. It's strange hearing those words, bearing the weight of them, and yet feeling like I'm still just the girl who once lived alone in a tower, stolen from everything she knew.

"I'm not sure I'm ready to be Luna," I admit, my voice meek.

Hanna's hands are gentle as she reaches for mine. "You're strong and resilient. You've been ready all along," she says firmly. She braids my hair, weaving in bluebells, violets, and bright fuchsia gathered from the valley. By the time the moon is high and full tonight, they'll glow like starlight threaded through my hair.

As she works, Mother pulls a delicate bracelet from a small velvet pouch—a circle of woven gold with a pendant shaped like an oak tree. She fastens it around my wrist. "For strength," she says. "For love."

"It's beautiful, Mother. Thank you."

The moonstone ring Leo gave me on my birthday rests on my finger, cool and familiar. He'd slipped it on my hand beneath the last full moon, calling it a promise and a beginning. I haven't taken it off since. Around my neck, I wear the necklace Leo gave me the night he proposed.

My mother holds the gown steady as I step into it. Hanna fastens the delicate pearl buttons that trail up my spine. The silk settles over my skin like a whisper—cool, smooth, impossibly light. The fitted bodice hugs my waist before flowing into wispy layers. When they step back, I turn toward the mirror.

For a moment, I just stare. The girl in the reflection looks radiant —wrapped in white and moonlight.

My mother smiles, misty-eyed. Hanna squeezes my hand. "You look like a Luna," she says.

From just outside we hear the string quartet playing a ballad Leo chose. Lorna stands, moving toward the entrance. "It's time," she says gently.

"The moonstones in your crown sparkle as you move," Hanna whispers. "You look so elegant and regal."

I step out of the tent. Moonbeam Valley is alive with light and song, bathed in silver and golden hues that shine like a dream. The full moon hangs high, a guardian watching over us as the evening air hums with magic.

Thousands of shifters, both human and wolf forms, gather beneath ancient trees draped in glowing vines and flowers that pulse with a gentle light. Lanterns float like stars caught in the branches, casting warm light over faces filled with joy and awe.

The music rises on the breeze, strings in bright harmony born of the packs united. It carries across the valley, a celebration of love and new beginnings.

I walk down the aisle among friends and family, and stand beside Leo at the wood carved altar, our hands intertwined, our hearts beating steadily in the quiet that settles before the ceremony. His dark eyes hold mine, steady and fierce, and I feel a calm I never thought possible.

Around us, the crowd stretches wide, each pack in their finest, our colors vibrant under the stars. The valley sparkles with enchantment, a promise sealed by old rites and whispered blessings.

Hanna's voice carries as she begins to sing.

"By moon and river, by fire and earth,

Two souls entwined in love's true worth.

Beneath the gaze of Luna's light,

We join these hearts on this sacred night."

The magic in the air deepens, swirling through the trees and over the gathered packs, threading through every heart and soul.

Near the altar, in front of the High Priest, Leo steps forward. His voice is low but clear. "Roxanna, you are my mate, my partner, my strength. I vow to stand by your side through every battle, to protect you, to cherish you, as long as the moon watches over us."

I squeeze his hand, my voice steady though my heart swells. "Leo, you are my home, my heart's true calling. With you, I am whole. I promise to walk beside you, through shadow and light, through all our days."

At the word of the High Priest, Leo pulls me close and kisses me deeply, as the packs howl around us—a wild, joyful chorus of acceptance and love, echoing through the valley.

As the howls fade into the night sky, Leo laces his fingers through mine and grins, his eyes full of fire.

The crowd moves. Laughter, music, the scent of roasted meat and peach wine fill the air. Lanterns sway overhead as we lead the way toward the feast, our first steps as mates not just honored, but celebrated. The ceremony may be over, but the night has only just begun.

The music swells, and Leo pulls me close. We move onto the dance floor beneath the stars—our first dance as wedded mates.

Around us, laughter and song, friends old and new, swirl together. Marek and Hanna weave through the crowd. Silas, Corwin, Briar, and Harla share stories beneath the boughs.

Fireworks burst above, sparks flying and twisting in the sky like living stars, bathing the valley in color and light.

Children chase each other through the grass, splash in the brook, and take rides on the merry-go-round.

I rest my head against Leo's shoulder, the warmth of his body grounding me, and I know that this—this moment—is everything.

We belong together.

Leo's hand is warm in mine as we move through the crowd, greeting friends and family. Marek's booming laugh carries from where he's talking with Silas and Corwin near the feast tables piled high with fruits, the elk from our hunt roasted to perfection, fresh bread, and sweet pastries.

Hanna is charming a group of small children, serving them lemonade and candied lemons, her radiant smile lighting up the night. I catch her eye, and she winks, pleased with how everything is unfolding.

"Come," Leo says, guiding me toward a circle of familiar faces. Kianna, Briar, and Harla wave us over, their expressions bright with happiness. They have that easy camaraderie that only comes from shared battles and long friendship.

The music shifts to a faster rhythm that sends people spinning and swirling in joyous dance. Some leap into the air as their wolf forms flash briefly beneath the moonlight, wild and free.

I laugh, swept up in the pure joy around me, and for a moment, I forget the dark days we've left behind. Here, now, there is only light and hope.

Leo pulls me closer.

"I can't believe this is where the tower used to stand," I say.

He nods, his eyes meeting mine. "Now look at what you've made of it. It's beautiful. You took something painful and turned it into a blessing."

I smile, leaning into him. "It's our new beginning."

Nearby, my mother and father stand together, their faces beaming with pride. They've fully embraced the celebration, laughing and sharing stories with members of every pack.

I catch Mother's eye, and she waves me over. We join hands, her grip strong and steady.

"I'm so proud of you, Roxanna," she says softly. "You've taken something broken and turned it into a place for all of us."

Her words settle as comfort and pride in my chest.

Leo steps forward, catching Father's attention. The two men exchange a firm nod—allies in leadership and respect.

As the night deepens, the revelry grows wilder. More guests shift into their wolf forms in celebration, their howls joining the music in a hauntingly beautiful chorus. Children dart through the crowd, their laughter ringing like bells. Platters pass between packs, sharing food and stories. Toasts rise, and glasses clink in warmth and friendship.

Hanna pulls me aside, her eyes shining. "This is only the beginning, Roxy. You and Leo—together—you'll lead us to something stronger than ever."

I nod, squeezing her hand. "I'm so grateful for your faith and friendship."

Leo sweeps me into another dance, spinning me beneath a canopy of red roses. His touch is gentle but sure, a promise and a comfort all at once.

As the celebration carries on, I realize something deep and true—I have found my place. Not just in this valley, or among these packs, but beside Leo, as his mate, as a leader. The witches are banished. The valley is alive with hope, and tonight, we are free.

When the last fireworks fade, and the music lowers to a gentle hum, I sit beside Leo on a blanket under the trees, wrapped in his arms.

The stars are scattered thick above us, the moon a glowing crown over the valley. Lanterns sway in the trees, casting golden halos on the revelers still dancing beneath them. It's all a blur of happiness, but now, the moment has come.

Leo finds my hand and squeezes gently. I look up at him, my Alpha, and everything inside me swells with that impossible fullness I've felt all day. The music fades. Someone calls out an old, familiar note, and then, as if summoned, the crowd sings.

It's a traditional parting song—low and sweet at first, then rising in waves, layered with harmony in an ancient tongue. I don't know all the words, but I know what they mean. Blessings for the journey. For joy. For a love that lasts.

Leo steps behind me and wraps his arms around my waist, swaying with me for a breath, letting the sound wash over us. I close my eyes, sinking into the music, into him. Into us.

Then, we turn.

Two of the enchanted horses stand waiting, just beyond the line of lantern light–the lavender-blue mare who took to me first, and the sleek silver stallion who has followed Leo like a shadow for two days now. Their wings shimmer faintly even at rest, catching every flicker of firelight.

"They're ready," Leo murmurs beside me, his voice warm and full of wonder.

"So am I," I whisper back.

The crowd parts to let us through, still singing. Hanna tosses a handful of flower petals as we pass. Harla gives me a wave. Marek salutes Leo, his eyes uncharacteristically misty. Even Silas looks solemn.

We reach the edge of the clearing, and the horses bow their heads reverently. I run a hand along the mare's neck, her mane silken beneath my fingertips. She snorts and shifts her wings as if impatient for flight.

Leo helps me mount, his touch gentle but sure. He swings up onto the stallion in one smooth motion. I glance back once more at the lights, the laughter, the land we've built with so much hope, and then we take off.

The moment their hooves leave the ground, a cheer rises from the crowd below. I can still hear them singing as we ascend, their voices echoing through the valley, growing smaller and sweeter with distance, and then it's just us and the night sky.

Wind rushes past, cold, clean and wild. The horses fly swiftly and surely, their wings cutting through the night like neon sails. The world below shrinks away—fields, rivers, and forests blurring into shadow and mist.

Leo flies close, just a few feet away. His eyes are on me more than the sky, his smile bright and sure. *"You look like moonlight,"* he says through the mind-link.

"You look like you're trying to flirt while flying a magical beast."

He grins. *"Is it working?"*

"Yes," I admit with my heart pounding.

We fly higher, the air turning crisp and thin, until the lowlands disappear behind us, and the mountains rise ahead, snow-capped, massive, ancient. The moon casts a silver glow across the peaks, and the stars seem close enough to touch.

Nestled on a ridge is a tiny cottage, its roof dusted in snow, a wisp of smoke curling from the chimney. The windows gleam warmly, like it's been waiting just for us.

The horses glide low, circling once before landing gently on the packed snow. I slide down and immediately sink to my ankles, laughing. Leo is beside me in a second, catching my hand before I lose my balance.

The cottage was prepared by servants earlier this evening and smells of cedar and cinnamon. A fire crackles in the hearth, and thick quilts are folded at the foot of the bed. There's tea warming on the stove and two mugs waiting on the table.

Leo shuts the door behind us and turns to face me, his eyes searching mine.

"We made it," he says.

"Yes," I breathe. "We did."

And here, in this quiet place between sky and snow, the world narrows to just the two of us—still wearing our wedding clothes, still dizzy with joy. I don't know what tomorrow holds. But tonight, I am his, and he is mine, and that's all I need.

Leo takes my hand and draws me closer, his palm warm against mine, our wedding rings catching the firelight. He lifts my hand to his lips and kisses my knuckles. "You're so beautiful it hurts."

I smile, suddenly shy beneath the weight of his gaze. "You've seen me covered in mud and blood, Leo."

He chuckles. "Yeah, but I've never seen you like this. As my wife."

The words settle over us like a hush, sweet and solemn. My heart thuds as I take a step closer, rising on my toes to kiss him. Softly at first, his hands find my waist and pull me in, and the kiss deepens, slow and aching. His lips taste like the spiced cider from the celebration but also like him—warm, steady, mine.

My fingers slide into his hair. His hands roam gently over the fabric of my gown. I don't want to rush or to break the magic spell of this moment. We've waited so long and fought through so much. I want to feel every heartbeat of this night.

He lifts me easily, carries me to the bed, and lays me down with care. I reach for him, my breath catching when his lips brush my collarbone.

"I want you." I whisper.

He undresses me slowly and carefully. My gown slips away like falling petals, gathered on the floor. Then he undresses too, never looking away.

When he joins me on top of the blankets, his skin is warm against mine, his heart a steady rhythm beneath my palm. My hands roam across his chiseled muscles, sexy and sleek.

Leo's lips explore my curves, and my body writhes in pleasure. We move together, slowly at first, learning, delighting in each gasp, each shiver.

"Roxy," he murmurs. His voice breaks slightly. "I've never loved anyone the way I love you."

Tears prick my eyes. I kiss his shoulder, his jaw, his mouth. "You're my home," I breathe. "You always have been."

The world fades to nothing but this bed, this firelight, this love. He holds me like I'm something precious and touches me like he knows every inch of me already but still wants to learn more. We crash through waves of ecstasy together, over and over again.

Later, we lie tangled in the blankets, his arms around me and my head on his chest, and I close my eyes, my heart full. This is our beginning, and it's more than I ever dreamed.

THE BABY IN THE WOMB

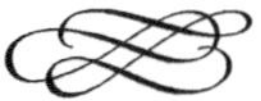

Roxy

One year later...

The sun spills through the windows of the healing cottage, dappled light warming the woven rugs and shelves of herbs. A breeze stirs the drying bundles above the hearth. It carries the scent of lavender, thyme, and sage. I sit on the low stool near the back wall, brushing out my hair with fingers slicked in oil. The strands shimmer faintly, like moonlight caught in motion, as they always do now.

A year ago, I was still learning what it meant to lead, to love, to live freely. Now, I'm something more. Still Luna, still Leo's mate, but now something ancient and revered: a healer; my gift from the Moon Goddess.

When I braid my hair around wounds, pain fades. Broken bones knit faster. The sick breathe easier. I don't fully understand it, but I trust it, and I know it's become my calling.

The door creaks open. I glance up as Hanna steps inside, her cheeks flushed from the walk up the hill. She's carrying a basket of berries, but her smile is brighter than the sun outside.

"I hope I'm not interrupting," she says.

"Never," I say, standing to greet her. "Sit down. I'll make tea."

But she waves a hand. "No tea yet. I have to tell you something." Her voice is breathless, and she sets the basket down with trembling fingers.

I raise an eyebrow, my heart fluttering with curiosity. "What is it?"

She crosses the room and grabs my hands, squeezing tight. "I'm going to have a baby."

My jaw drops. "You're—what?"

Tears shimmer in her eyes. "I am. I went to the midwife yesterday. I wasn't sure, but then she confirmed it this morning." She laughs, breathless. "Roxy, Marek and I have been trying for years. We nearly gave up."

I pull her into a tight hug, and she clings to me, burying her face against my shoulder. "I'm so happy for you," I whisper.

She pulls back just enough to meet my gaze. "And I think I know why it finally happened."

I tilt my head, confused.

"It was your hair," Hanna says, her voice softer now, thick with emotion.

I nod slowly. "You were having headaches. You couldn't sleep."

She gives a trembling smile. "That was only part of it. No matter what Marek and I tried before, it never worked. But after I started braiding your hair... the pain stopped. Something changed. I feel stronger, whole somehow. I didn't realize it then, but your gift—it healed me, Roxy."

A lump rises in my throat. I reach out and cup her face gently, both of us laughing now, half-crying. "That's the most beautiful thing I've ever heard."

She squeezes my hand. "And I'm going to need you when the little one comes. I'm terrified and overjoyed all at once."

"Well," I say slowly, "you won't be alone in parenting."

She frowns in confusion, but I don't make her wait long. I take a breath, then whisper, "I'm having a little one, too."

Hanna gasps. "Roxy!"

"I haven't told Leo yet," I admit, my hands instinctively brushing over my stomach. "I was waiting for the right moment. But I had to tell someone, and—"

She launches into another hug. "You told me. I'm honored."

We laugh again, holding each other tight in the quiet morning light, two future mothers surrounded by healing herbs and magic.

"Imagine," Hanna says, pulling back, "our pups growing up together. Causing trouble together."

"They'll be wild," I say with a grin. "And brave."

"And so very loved," she says.

We sit together, eating berries, our hands resting over our growing bellies, talking softly about all that comes next.

***

Our home smells like roasted goose, vegetables, and baking bread. I've laid the table with care: soft linen napkins, two silver plates, and the moonstone wine glasses we received as a wedding gift. Outside, I hear the crunch of boots on pebbles, and my heart skips.

I smooth my hands over my deep blue velvet dress, one of Leo's favorites, and check the table one last time before turning toward the door.

Leo steps inside, his dark hair tousled and damp. His cheeks are flushed from the wind, and he looks tired but content. When he sees me, something in his face softens instantly.

"You've already made dinner," he says, his eyes scanning the table. "And you look…" He trails off, walking toward me. "Like a dream."

"I thought you might be hungry," I say, stepping into his arms.

He pulls me close, wrapping me in his warmth. "Always. But this?" He kisses my cheek, then my jaw. "This is something else."

He pulls off his coat and joins me at the table. I pour us both a glass of sparkling cider. He raises his brow. "No wine tonight?"

I shake my head with a small smile. "Not tonight."

He doesn't press, just grins and takes a sip. "This smells incredible."

We eat together by firelight, laughter and warmth filling the room. Leo tells me about the hunt, how Silas nearly slipped off a frozen ledge and Marek made a bet he couldn't win. I watch him talk, soaking in the way he gestures with his hands, the gleam in his eyes. I've loved him in a hundred ways already, but tonight, I love him with something deeper—something new.

When our plates are empty, I stand and reach for his hand. "Come sit with me by the fire."

He lets me lead him to the thick rug where blankets and pillows are piled. He settles behind me, wrapping his arms around my waist, his lips brushing my neck. "What's all this?" he murmurs. "You've been planning something."

I nod. My heart is pounding. "I have."

He leans in, playful. "Is it a surprise for me?"

"Yes," I whisper, twisting to face him. I take his hands in mine and place them gently over my belly. I look up into his eyes, searching. "I found out a few days ago. We are going to have a baby, Leo."

His eyes flicker from my face to where my hands rest on my middle, then back again. "You're—? Are you sure?"

I nod, a smile breaking across my face. "I'm sure. I went to the midwife, and she confirmed it."

He stares at me for a moment, completely still, and then the joy hits him like lightning. He pulls me into his arms, cradling my head and burying his face against my hair. "You're going to be a mother," he murmurs. "And I'm going to be a father."

I laugh, breathless, blinking back tears. "We're going to have a pup, Leo."

He leans back just enough to look at me again, his eyes shining. "You're amazing," he says. "I didn't think I could love you more, but— Goddess, Roxy." Leo kisses me with more passion than ever before, causing my whole body to heat. "We'll raise our pup in a home filled with love," he says in a low voice. "With safety, and strength. With a mother who can heal anything, and a father who will never stop protecting them."

"You'll make an incredible father, Leo," I say softly, resting my head on his shoulder. I pause, smile faintly, and tilt my head toward the sounds outside. "Do you hear that?" I whisper.

He tilts his head. "The wind?"

"No." I smile. "Music from the village square."

Leo grins. "Sounds like another fiddle circle."

"It's hard to believe sometimes."

"What is?"

"That it's over," I say quietly. "The curses. The tower. The witches. All of it."

We fall silent for a while, watching the flames dance. Somewhere nearby, someone lets out a joyous howl. A moment later, another answers.

"Five packs," Leo says. "And not one of them fighting."

"Moon River, Golden Elm, Ravensong, Nightshade, Ebonlight." I name them aloud. "All working together. It's not just peace. It's… family."

Leo nods. "No more curses. No more vanished hunters. No more children growing up afraid."

I rest a hand on my belly, and his gaze follows it. "They'll be born into a different world," I say.

"Our world," he replies. "One we built together."

He leans in and kisses me, slow and sure, his forehead resting against mine afterward.

I close my eyes, feeling the fire, the love, the heartbeat beneath my hand.

Our beginning.

Thank you for reading! Cinderella's story is coming soon!

ALSO BY BELLA MOONDRAGON

The Alpha King's Breeder series:

Bought by the Alpha: The Alpha King's Breeder Book 1

Loved by the Alpha: The Alpha King's Breeder Book 2

Lost by the Alpha: The Alpha King's Breeder Book 3

Luna of the Alpha: The Alpha King's Breeder Book 4

Legacy of the Alpha: The Alpha Kings's Breeder Book 5

Daughter of the Alpha: The Alpha King's Breeder Book 6

Descendants of the Alpha: The Alpha King's Breeder Book 7

Shadow of the Alpha: The Alpha King's Breeder Book 8

Son of the Alpha: The Alpha King's Breeder Book 9

Spare of the Alpha: The Alpha King's Breeder Book 10

Claimed by the Alpha: The Alpha King's Breeder Book 11

Atonement for the Alpha King: The Alpha King's Breeder Book 12

Rejected by the Alpha: The Alpha King's Breeder Book 13

Abducted by the Alpha: The Alpha King's Breeder Book 14

Wolf Shifter Fairy Tale Retellings series

Beauty and the Alpha Beast

Sleeping Beasty

Tangling With the Alpha

The Luna's Vampire Prince series:

The Culling

The Kingdom

The Conquered

Pregnant With Four Alphas' Babies

Chosen As the Breeder

Mated to Four Alphas

Threats Against the Breeder

At War for the Breeder

The Stolen Breeder

Four Alphas, Four Babies

Becoming the Luna Queen

Descendants of the Breeder

Desired by the Devil series

Whispers of the Devil

Banter of the Devil

Murmurs of the Devil

The Mafia Kings series

Indebted to the Mafia King

<u>Loved by the Mafia King</u>

Claimed by the Mafia King

Secrets of the Mafia King

Burned by the Mafia King

Kidnapped by the Mafia King (coming soon!)

Dark Stalker Romance series

Tempted by Sin

Fated to Sin

Secret Billionaires series

Finding the Secret Billionaire by Olivia Bhelle Kildare

Falling for My Secret Billionaire by Bella Moondragon

Driven by the Secret Billionaire by ID Johnson

Wolf Shifter Alpha Kings series

Ravens and Ruins

Sundrops and Shadows

Snowflakes and Sabotage

The Vampire King's Feeder series

Claiming the Alpha's Daughter

Loving the Alpha's Daughter

Finding the Alpha's Daughter

Bewitching the Alpha's Son (coming soon!)

Writing as B. Moon

The Boy Who Died

Sign up for Bella's newsletter here.

Or get a free novella from The Alpha King's Breeder series when you sign up here:
The Beta and the Maid

Follow Bella on Facebook here.

Follow Bella on Bookbub here.